Life the Future Smiles Upon
- Self-sufficiency in the AI Age

未来向我们微笑的人生
～人工智能时代的自给自足～

森 孝之

「プロローグ」 〜わたしの使命〜

　「これは辛い」と思って目が覚めました。明るくて広い屋内でした。さまざまな体型や服装の高齢者が、車椅子などの介護具に頼り、姿形が揃った制服姿の若い男女の世話になっていたのです。よく見ると、そこはまるで生身の人のように見えるアンドロイド・汎用型 AI ロボットが立ち働く介護施設でした。

　工業文明の黎明期は、機械が普及するに従って、農業文明が生み出した奴隷の解放が進み、アメリカでは劇的な事例さえ生み出しました。近年では、ロボットが普及する世の中になり、工業文明が生み出したホワイトカラーやブルーカラーの削減（リストラ）を進めています。だが、この削減は解放とは受け止められないし、物的に豊かな社会になりながら劇的な事例は見られません。それはどうしてか。

　この疑問と備えで私の生涯は終りそうです。戦時中の都会から田舎への幼児期の疎開に始まり、中学時代は結核菌に侵され、一旦は就職や結婚を諦めました。しかし、ストレプトマシンなどの抗生物質の発明に救われ、生き残れただけでなく、今や多くの人々が悠々自適の日々を過ごしているかのように見て下さいます。

　それは、貧富格差がはなはだしい世の中になったせいもあるでしょう。これは、特化型 AI ロボットなどをシステム的に活かす人々と、そのシステムが生み出すモノ、サービス、あるいは職場などに魅了され、群がった人々との間に生じた格差と見て良さそうです。だが、私はこのいずれでもなく、わが道の創出に努めたのです。「古人の知恵」と「近代科学の成果物」を組み合わせた生き方ですが、それが次第に「未来が微笑みかけてくる生き方」のように感じさせるようになったのです。

　ここに至る過程で、こうした時々の想いをコラムなどに綴って来ましたが、振り返ってみるとその想いは一貫していたように思われます。

〜わたしの使命（2001 年 7 月 5 日）〜

　1947 年の今日、わが国初の経済白書が発行された。その後、地固めの時、先進国への道、能率と福祉の向上、豊かさへの挑戦など、様々な副題がついた白書が世に送り出された。その間に、私は子どもから成人へ、経済界から今の立場へと身の置

きどころが変わった。世の中もめまぐるしく変わり、便利で豊かな世の中になった。

　風呂や冷暖房も指先一本で用が足せる。無洗米が現れてご飯も指先一本で炊ける。衣服や家、あるいは旅行などもプロが考えて打ち出す既製品を選り好みさえすれば済む世の中になった。とはいえ私たちは何か大きな忘れ物をしていたような気がしてならない。

　学生時代に工業デザインを学んだ私は、商社時代にその手法でファッションを囃したことがある。今はその目で世の中を見つめ直し、今後の進むべき方向を後進に指し示さなければならない立場にある。振り返ってみれば、これまでのデザインは豊かで便利な世の中にする上で貢献したが、気がかりな問題にもかかわっていたように思う。デザインは経済学や科学などが進んだところで発達したが、そうした国や地域ほど環境破壊、資源枯渇、生活習慣病、あるいは野生動植物の絶滅などの諸問題と深く関わってきた。これからはこうした諸問題の解消に役立つ方向へとベクトルを改め、新たなる繁栄の道を模索しなければならない。

　そうした新たな繁栄を目指し、そこで有用となる若人の教育を目標として掲げ、教職員が一つとなって教育活動に当たる学校に私はしたい。それが、地域社会への貢献を標榜する学校の学長にとって最も大切な課題ではないか。

（岐阜新聞「素描」20010705、原題「わたしの夢」）

　こうした想いを打ち出すたびに、私は己の生き方に弾みをつけてきたように思います。それはおのずと、工業文明に次ぐ新しい文明の姿を心に描き、次の時代が許容するに違いないと信じる生き方の根本と精神の追求になりました。

　今や傘寿となり、持病にもさいなまれる私ですが、これらのコラムの幾つかを選び出し、多少加筆して一書にまとめることにしました。なぜなら、それが破たんしつつある工業文明に翻弄されず、汎用型 AI ロボットを上手に使いこなし、次代を先取りしながら心豊かに暮らすヒントになりそうだ、と思われてならないからです。

Prologue - My Mission

"This is terrible," I thought and then woke up. It was a large, bright interior. Elderly people situated in wheelchairs in assorted conditions and dress were being cared for by young men and women in matching uniforms. Upon closer inspection, this turned out to be an elder care facility run by generic-use AI robots all of which looked practically human.

At the dawn of industrial civilization, increased use of machinery and the dramatic events of the American Civil War moved society to the abolition of slavery in that agrarian era. Likewise, in recent years as an outcome of industrial civilization, we have seen an increase in the use of technology throughout the world which has led to a "restructuring" or gradual disappearance of both white and blue collar workers.

Yet the attenuation of these workers is not perceived as freedom for them, nor have any dramatic events, which usually accompany an increasingly materialistic society, occurred in response to this gradual disappearance. The question is why is this so?

I suspect I will go to my grave with deep reservations and provisions for this issue. I was evacuated to the countryside during WWII when I was a child, and then contracted tuberculosis during middle school, so at one point I gave up on ever getting a proper job or getting married. Yet, I survived thanks to the discovery of antibiotics like streptomycin. I went from despair and depression to a life some people might even see as a life of leisure.

My rise to a comfortable life may be in part due to the stark discrepancy between the haves and the have-nots nowadays. This is most likely the gap between those who systematically make use of specialized AI technology and the many who have been entranced by those products, services and workplaces that the system produces. Rather than joining one of these camps, however, I have worked hard to create a pathway which combines the "wisdom of the ancients" and the "deliverables of modern science." I have gradually come to feel that this is "the way of life the future will smile upon." I have set down thoughts about this process over the years in various newspaper columns, and looking back on them, I see this one consistent conviction throughout.

My Mission as the President of a College
(The Gifu News: "A Rough Outline" July 5, 2001, Title: "My Dream")

It was on this day in 1947 when Japan issued its first economic white paper. Subsequently, when our country was setting down its new foundations, a variety of white papers were published with subtitles such as "The path to becoming an advanced country", "Improvements in efficiency and welfare", and "Championing the cause of a better life". In those years as Japan was developing, I too grew from childhood to adulthood, and transitioned from the business world to being an educator. The world, as well, transformed dramatically, replete with convenience and affluence.

Now, the world is full of conveniences such as a Japanese deep tub which can be heated with the touch of a button, and air conditioning on demand. There is even rice that requires no pre-washing, and can be cooked by just the touch of a finger. We find ourselves in a world in which we can get away with simply choosing a manufactured product we like from among commodities like clothing, homes, or even travel options designed and marketed by professionals. However, I feel as if something of significance is being forgotten here.

I studied industrial design in college, and when I was working for a trading company, there was a time when I bought into and applauded the fashion world. Now, I am in a position to reexamine that world with what I have learned along the way, and counsel younger people about the right direction for the future. Upon reflection, design, as we have known it up to this point, contributed to making the world more abundant and convenient; but there are troubling issues that come into play here. Design as a discipline advances where there is progress in economics and science. Yet, the more advanced a country or region becomes the more intricate are the many associated problems such as environmental destruction, depletion of natural resources, lifestyle-related illnesses, and the extinction of wild plants and animals. We must re-calibrate the vector of our current heading to solve such multifaceted problems, and seek a new path to prosperity.

I wish to make this institution one in which the faculty and staff engage as one in educational activities with the goal of guiding young people toward the target of this new prosperity. This is, without a doubt, the most important issue for the head of a college which advocates contributing to the regional community.

Every time I put my thoughts down on paper, I feel even more fortified in the commitment to my personal way of life. It comes down to imagining in my mind, first, my true self and the new civilization which will succeed industrial civilization; and two, the pursuit of the foundations and spirit of the life granted to us by the next age. I have reached my 80th birthday, and though I live with a variety of health challenges, I have decided that it is time for me to compile, with some editing, a few columns I have written in the past. Now, more than ever, rather than being led around by the nose by the pretenses of our industrial civilization, which is clearly on the decline, I feel it is important to share wisdom about prudent use of general-use AI technology as well as tips for staying ahead of the curve, and living a spiritually rich life.

序言～我的使命～

从梦里醒来，心情极其沉重！在梦里我看到一个宽敞明亮的房间，体型不同身穿各色服装的老人们借助轮椅等护理器具生活在那里，几个身穿制服姿态完全相同的青年男女在照顾他们。仔细一看，虽然这些人的长相和真人没有太大的不同，但是马上明白过来，原来这里是一所通用型人工智能机器人工作的养老院。

工业文明的黎明期，机械的普及逐渐解放了农业文明的牺牲（奴隶）。近年机器人的普及同样使工业文明的产物"白领和蓝领"被消减（解雇）了不少。但是这个消减却不能解释成解放劳动者，那为什么呢？

我的一生可能会带着这个疑问，在为此做准备的过程中谢幕。这一生曾经从战时幼小的我离开城市去农村避难开始，中学时代患了肺结核，一段时间失去对就职和结婚的信心。可是链菌素等抗生素的发明挽救了我，在很多人的眼里认为我现在的生活过得悠闲自在。

这也许是因为近来社会上的贫富之差越来越大。我认为这个差距源于活用特化型人工智能机器人等系统的人和沉醉在出自这些系统的物品、服务、以及工作上的人。我不属于这两者，我有自己的目标，努力走我那条以古人的智慧和近代科学的成果合为一体的道路。从此在脑里开始描绘"未来向我们微笑的人生"。

至今的道路曲折坎坷，有时把这些感慨写成文章。总的回想起来，自己的想法始终是具有一贯性的。

～我的使命（2001年7月5日）～

1947年，我国发行了第一本经济白皮书。以后为了打好基础，走上先进国家的道路，提高能率和福祉，富有挑战等带着各种各样副题的白皮书相继出世。在这期间，我从儿时迈向成人，自己的立场也从经济界转换到现在。世界发生了急剧的变化，让我们生活在便利富有的社会。

洗澡和空调只要用手指按一下就能调好。自从市场出现"免淘米"，做饭也一样省事了。生活中的衣/食/住以及旅行等，只要从各界专家想好的既成品中挑选自己喜欢的产品就可以。即使这样，我还是觉得好像失去了什么重要的东西。

学生时代我学的是工业设计，商社时代用此手法尝试过服饰。现在用这双眼睛观察社会，站在应该指示后辈人今后前进方向的立场。回顾自身，我的设计为建设方便富有的社会做出了贡献，同时也参与了令人担心的社会问题。它在经济学和科学的发展中成熟，这些国家和地域相对来说，在破坏环境、浪费资源、生活习惯病、以及野生动植物灭绝等问题上都有密切的关连。今后为了有益解决这些问题而改变矢量，应该摸索新的繁荣之路。

这样以建设新的繁荣为目标，举起"教育前途无量的年轻人"的旗帜，我的愿望是让学校全体教职员团结一致，共同开展教育活动。那才是作为以贡献地域社会为标榜的大学校长的最大课题。

（2001年7月5日岐阜报"素描"原题"我的梦想"）

每当我提出自己的这些想法，自己的人生好像也被它激励。这样我不断追求工业文明以后的新文明，相信我追求的人生根本和精神一定是下个时代可以容许的。

今年我八十大寿，日语叫"伞寿"（因为"伞"字是由"八和十"两字组成的）。虽然身患扩张型心肌病，还是选了几篇文章，又添了一些内容，决定出这本书。因为我觉得它能让人们不被逐渐瓦解的工业文明所捉弄，给方便使用通用型人工智能机器人，走在下个文明前边的人们一些心灵上的提示。

未来が微笑みかける生き方 〜 AI 時代の自給自足 〜

目次

「プロローグ」 〜わたしの使命〜 2

1章　AI時代に備える12のヒント 14

 1. オリジナルを尊ぶ 14
 2. プリンシプルを見定める 14
 3. 謙虚にチェンジマインドする 15
 4. コミュニケーションを尊ぶ気概を育む 16
 5. 自己責任の範囲を広げる 16
 6. 足るを知る 17
 7. 本当のソロバンをはじく 18
 8. 価値を創造する 18
 9. 相互扶助を心がける 19
 10. 小さな巨人を目指そう 20
 11. 美意識や価値観を見直す 20
 12. 清豊を目指す 21

2章　未来が微笑みかける生き方 36

3章　「アイトワ 12 節」〜同じ心と出会うまで〜 43

第1節　スプートニクの打ち上げ
　　　病気と受験の失敗で落胆する私 44
第2節　太陽が鼓舞した自立の夢 45
第3節　樹と夢の種をまいた 46
第4節　大学卒業を目前に、決意を固める 47
第5節　恵まれた仕事　それでも私は使命を貫く 48
第6節　使命その1　住宅ローン 49
第7節　両親もこの地に移り住む 50
第8節　人生を変えたアポロ8号からの光景
　　　地球は私たちの唯一の棲家 52
第9節　同じ心と出会う　人形工房 53

4章　家屋を「生産の場」から「創造の場」に高める 54

5章　「アイトワ12節」〜妻と支え合いながら〜 58

第10節　創作空間をつくる 58
第11節　1986年、アイトワの誕生 59
第12節　エコライフ実践者に引き継ぐまで、................60
　　　　薪を割り続ける

6章　アイトワの時空 62

1. アイトワのシンボルマーク 62
2. エコライフガーデン（アイトワの庭）................64
3. エコライフガーデンでのこぼれ話 67

7章　未来の夢 73

1. アイトワを創出した想い 73
2. 未来の夢 74

アイトワでの思い出　エリザベス・アームストロング 83

「エピローグ」〜清豊を夢見て〜 86

あとがき 92

9

Life the Future Smiles Upon - Self-sufficiency in the AI Age

┃ contents

Prologue - My Mission 4

1章 Wisdom for the Era of Artificial Intelligence: 12 Lessons 22

Lesson 1 Honor the Original 22
Lesson 2 Determining Principles 22
Lesson 3 Change Your Mind With Humility 23
Lesson 4 Teaching "Grit" 24
Lesson 5 Enlarge Your Sphere of Responsibility 24
Lesson 6 How Much is Enough? 25
Lesson 7 A Real Abacus 26
Lesson 8 Create Value 26
Lesson 9 Mindful of Mutual Support 27
Lesson 10 Little Giants 28
Lesson 11 Rethinking Aesthetics and Values 28
Lesson 12 Noble Wealth 29

2章 Life the Future Smiles Upon 38

3章 Twelve Views of aightowa: Encounters with those of like mind 43

First View Sputnik launched.
Sick and failing, I became despondent. 44
Second View Dream of self-sufficiency inspired by the sun. ...45
Third View Planted trees and seeds of dreams. 46
Fourth View Firm resolve at the end of college. 47
Fifth View Desirable job. Still faithful to destiny. 48
Sixth View Step One: House loan. 49
Seventh View Parents chose to live here too. 50
Eighth View Life-changing view from Apollo 8:
Earth, our one home. 52
Ninth View More like-minded people. Doll atelier. 53

4章 Elevate Your Home from a Place of "Production" to One of "Creativity" 54

5章 Twelve Views of **aightowa**: Mutual Support in our Marriage 58

Tenth View Construction of creative space. 58

Eleventh View Birth of **aightowa**, 1986. 59

Twelfth View Chopping wood until the next generation of Eco-lifers takes over. 60

6章 The **aightowa** Cosmos 62

1. **aightowa**'s Logo 62
2. Eco-garden (**aightowa**'s garden) 64
3. Eco-garden Fun Facts 67

7章 The Future Dream 76

1. Concepts Which Gave Rise to **aightowa** 76
2. The Future Dream 77

Memories of **aightowa**   Elizabeth Armstrong 82

Epilogue - The Dream of Noble Wealth 88

Afterword 93

未来向我们微笑的人生～人工智能时代的自给自足～

▌篇目

序言～我的使命～ 6

1章 准备迎接人工智能时代的 12 个启示 30

    1 尊重独创性 30
    2 要看清原理 30
    3 谦虚地转换思想 31
    4 注重交流 培养气概 31
    5 扩大自我责任的范围 32
    6 知足者常乐 32
    7 打真正的算盘 33
    8 创造价值 33
    9 注意相互扶助 34
   10 做个小巨人 34
   11 重新树立审美观和价值观 35
   12 以"清丰"为目标 35

2章 未来向我们微笑的人生 40

3章 爱永远农园 12景～找到志同道合的伴侣～ 43

第1景 发射人工卫星
        因疾病和高考失败而沮丧 44
第2景 太阳鼓舞我自立的梦想 45
第3景 播下树木和梦想的种子 46
第4景 在大学毕业以前下了一大决心 47
第5景 条件优越的工作也没有阻止我完成使命 48
第6景 第一个使命 贷款盖房 49
第7景 父母也来此同住 50
第8景 从阿波罗 8 号宇宙飞船看到的景观
        ～地球是我们唯一的住处～ 52
第9景 相遇知音 人偶制作室 53

4章 　将住房从"生产的场所"提高到"创意的场所"...54

5章 　爱永远农园 12 景～与妻子同心协力～ 58

　第10景 　建立创作空间 58

　第11景 　1986 年 　爱永远农园的诞生 59

　第12景 　等待实践环保生活的接班人
　　　　　 我会坚持劈柴耕地 60

6章 　爱永远农园的时空 62

　1. "爱永远农园"的标志 62

　2. 爱永远农园的庭院 64

　3. 爱永远农园庭院的花絮 67

7章 　未来的梦想 79

　我为什么创建"爱永远农园" 79

　未来的梦想 80

爱永远农园的回忆 　伊利莎白 阿姆斯特朗 84

结尾～生态文明的梦想～ 90

后记 94

1章　AI時代に備える12のヒント

1. オリジナルを尊ぶ（2005年8月19日）

　どうしてこんなものを買ってしまったのかとか、あんなことをしてしまったのかとくよくよしたことはありませんか。その連続だった私は、自活力を高めることでこうした後悔を減らせたように思います。

　反省や後悔を伴う失敗を振り返るうちに、その共通点に気づかされました。不安や劣等感などにさいなまれ、虚勢を張ったり判断力を欠いたりしていたのです。要は確かな自分のモノサシ（判断基準）を持たず、周りに振り回されていたのです。

　そこで、自分のモノサシや座標軸を見定め、それらを守り通す癖を身につけ、プリンシプルを明らかにしようとしています。とはいえ、世の中で首をかしげられるようなことはよくないので、たとえば所帯を構える時は、次のような事を願いました。

　「生涯を通してキミの手料理を幾度食べられるか。キミが洗ったYシャツを幾度着られるか。それをボクの幸せのバロメーターにしたい」など。

　「お袋の味」のように、勝手に世界一だと決めつけて悦に入ることにしたわけです。こうした気ままであればプライバシーの範囲内でしょう。だから社会の顰蹙をかわずに済むはずだ、と考えたわけです。もちろん妻には負担をかけたようですが、やがて妻の塩加減や洗濯の糊加減が私には一番心地よいものになりました。

　次第にモノサシの対象は広がり、既製品を選り好みする生き方では満足できなくなり、道具を駆使する手作り率を高めました。それが次第に自活力を高めさせ、わが道を、つまりオリジナル性の高い生き方を手に入れさせたように思います。同時に、それらが自分なりのモノサシや座標軸を固めさせたようで、くよくよすることが極端に減っています。

（産経新聞コラム「自活のススメ」20050819「幸せのバロメーター」）

2. プリンシプルを見定める（1995年10月14日）

　1962年に私は社会人になりましたが、就職先を決める時に大変迷っています。緑豊かな田園地帯から通える範囲内で探すか、引っ越す覚悟で探すかで迷ったわけです。候補にあげた勤め先はいずれも大都会にありました。高度経済成長が始まったばかりのころですから、大都会は緑どころではなく、大阪などは「煙の都」を売り物（繁栄のシンボル）にしていました。

　結局私は、京都の自宅から通勤が可能な大阪の総合商社を選びました。ですから、面接では、「転勤命令を出すのは会社の勝手でしょうが、そのときは私は勝手に辞めさせてもらいます」と発言しています。にもかかわらず、二百数十人の男子新入社員の一人にしてもらえたのです。

　入社翌年、私は両親の家よりもさらに奥まった山のすそ野に、住宅金融公庫を活か

し、小さな家を建てました。現在の住所です。週末は庭仕事に没頭する生き方が始まったわけです。

この緑豊かなくらし（野良仕事や造園）を守らせてくれる会社に感謝し、仕事に励みました。人並み以上に仕事はできたと思っています。

その後、さまざまなことがありましたが、この一つの住まいから離れることなく今日にいたっています。裏を返せば、緑豊かな土地に縛りつけられた人生といえなくもありません。

どうして緑に縛られたのだろうかと考えたこともあります。たぶん、今は亡き父の影響だと思います。病床にあった父は、なれない農作業で一家を支える母を助けるために、小学校に入ったばかりの私に20羽の鶏を、中学生になるとヤギを飼わせました。それが一家の大切なタンパク源となり、子どもなりに私は（食物連鎖に目覚め）植物の大切さを学んでいます。

その後、私はこの緑豊かな環境から離れておらず、自分たちの出す屎尿や生ごみなどを肥料として植物を育む庭仕事を守ってきました。

大学で色彩論を学んだことも関係していたかもしれません。緑の効能を教わったときのことを今でもよく覚えています。私たちの身体は、緑にとり囲まれていると心拍数や血圧が下がり、ホルモンの排出量が減り、時間の経過を緩慢に感じるようになる。だから逆に、ファストフード店や即席食品の包装など人の気持ちをせかせたりたかぶらせたりする場合は、赤やだいだい色などの暖色を多用しているのでしょう。

思い返せば、就職するときに迷ったのが良かったと思います。私はプリンシプル（原則）の大切さに気付かされたからです。その後、私は緑豊かな空間やそこで過ごす時間、あるいは道具を駆使する生き方を優先し、その逆のケースから遠ざかっています。それが次第に自活力を高めさせ、自分らしい暮らしを手に入れさせたように思われてなりません。

（朝日新聞コラム「くらし考」19951014、
原題「緑の土地に縛られる私」）

3. 謙虚にチェンジマインドする （2001年8月30日）

1962年（今から56年昔）の今日、キューバ危機という国家の存亡問題にかかわっていたケネディ大統領は、記者会見で、ある著作を読破し、ある指示も出したことを明らかにしています。

その年の春から総合商社に勤めていた私は、個人所得で5倍、乗用車の普及率では25倍ものスケールのアメリカを羨み、仕事に励んでいました。その後、日本は四半世紀ほどで追いつきますが、肝心かなめのものを次々と見過ごしていたようです。その顕著な1つが、その後の世界を大きく変えることになったこの著作でしょう。

勤めた商社にはアメリカ駐在員が大勢いました。私は衣料関係の仕事に携わり、手広くファッション業界とかかわっていました。しかし、当時アメリカで大きな物議をかもしていたこの著作にだれ一人として関心を示していません。今にして思えば、私たちは目先の利益や流行を追うことには執心しながら、意識の転換を迫る提言には鈍感だった、と見てよいのではないでしょうか。

その後アメリカでは、老若男女を対象とする衣料を打ち出したギャップ社は、やがてアメリカンズ・ベイシックウエアーを標榜し、創業30年で一兆円企業になっていま

1章　AI時代に備える12のヒント　15

す。アウトドアスポーツ衣料のパタゴニア社は、社会を改革する道具として企業を再生し、より良き地球環境を次世代に引き継ぐことを企業の使命に据えています。こうした動きの背景に、人々の意識や時代の潮流を変え、環境問題の古典として輝くことになるこの著作、レイチェル・カーソンの「沈黙の春」が見え隠れしています。

今日、わが国は閉塞感にさいなまれています。私はまずこうした意識の転換を迫る提言に謙虚となり、旧弊の払拭と新潮流の特定に努めることにしたい、と願っています。その手始めに、この著作の再読から始めよう。

（岐阜新聞コラム「素描」20010830、
原題「意識の転換」）

4. コミュニケーションを尊ぶ気概を育む（2006年1月20日）

アメリカで取引があった企業幹部の家庭では、息子のリッキーに月ぎめのお小遣いなど与えていませんでした。一人息子はお金を、労働の対価として両親から得ていたのです。

リッキーは、両親が家を空け「留守番をする日は稼ぎ時だ」と話していました。たとえば、鉢植え植物に水をやって枯らさなければ、母親から日決めの対価がもらえるなど。

その親子によれば、親子だという理由で定額のお小遣いをやりとりする話を近隣では聞かない、と話していました。女の子には子守りなど、その子にできそうな仕事を親子間や近隣間で与え合い、責任を持たせて稼ぎ出させていたわけです。

週末に招かれた日のことでした。父の帰りを待ち受けていたリッキーが、これまで通りに「車を洗わせて欲しい」と父に願い出ました。しかし父は、その願いを受け付

けず、即座に息子を車に乗せて出かけようとしました。そこで私は、同道を願い出たのです。父が息子に何をしようとしているのかを知りたかったわけです。

行き先はガソリンスタンドでした。父は洗車を依頼し、対価を支払うところを小さな息子に見せました。どうやら父が息子に支払っていた洗車代とガソリンスタンドで支払った対価は同額であったようです。

帰路、父は息子に問いかけました。「リッキーならどちらに頼むだろうか」と。ガソリンスタンドでの洗車と息子の洗車の仕上がり具合を自ら比較させ、選ぶ立場に立たせたのです。「もちろん」と父は付け加えました。出来栄えが同じなら、「私はリッキーを優先したい」。すかさず息子は「お父さん、もう一度ボクにチャンスをくれ」と頼んだのです。

（産経新聞コラム「自活のススメ」20060120、
原題「責任感とお小遣い」）

5. 自己責任の範囲を広げる（2005年1月28日）

学力の低下が問題になったり医療ミスの問題が多発したりしていますが、今日流の学力の向上で医療ミスの問題も解消できるのでしょうか。

わが家では心豊かな生活を夢見て自活力

の向上に努めていますが、それは自己責任能力を高め、その範囲を拡げることだと思っています。ですから医療のようにどうしても他の人の手をわずらわせることは、いわば分身を見定めて命を委ねるような覚悟と

態度で臨むことにしています。

　私はこの10年あまりの間に両親をなくしましたが、ともに掛かりつけの町医者の世話になりました。もとより医療はミスや技量不足の問題が伴いがちだし、それが深刻な後悔の原因になりそうです。ですから私たち夫婦は、最新の器機や設備とか最高の技術などを優先するよりも、たとえ失策が生じてもこの人ならむしろ「気苦労をおかけした」と気遣いたくなる医者を優先したわけです。

　これを人柄の問題だとすれば、今日の学力の向上はこの人柄の向上に焦点を絞っているようには見えませんから、不安です。それは、人間をマニュアル通りに扱える対象と考えたり人体を部品の寄せ集めからできた機械のように見たり、あるいは偏差値で人格まで推し量れそうに思ったりする社会風潮が生じさせた弊害ではないでしょうか。

　インフルエンザをこじらせた父だけでなく、大腸癌で小さな病院に入院した母も最期は自宅で、自分の布団での療養を望みました。そこで、分身と思う町医者や院長に往診してもらいながら家族の責任の下に介護する覚悟を決めました。きっと両親も心安らかに息を引き取ってくれたはずですが、なによりも私たちは思い残すことのない別れが出来ました。

（産経新聞コラム「自活のススメ」20050128、
原題「本当の学力とは」）

6. 足るを知る（2007年1月12日）

　神戸にあった中堅企業で社長室長をしていた時に、婚期を迎えた多くの若者が会社の低利住宅ローンを求めて席を訪ねて来ました。その都度私は、同じ大金を投じるなら、なるだけ広い土地を手に入れるなど私生活の充実に努めてはどうか、と提案しています。

　私生活が充実しておれば、多少仕事が過酷でも、健康的な任務でさえあれば耐えられそうに思います。ですから若者に、配偶者と自分自身の性格などに配慮した人生目標を早く見定め、たとえば陶芸が好みなら燃料にする木の苗木を植えておくなど、なるだけ早く手を打つべきだと勧めたのです。

　当時の私は、会社の近くに小さなマンションを手当てしており、ウイークデイはそこに泊まり、週末は京都にある私生活の拠点に帰り、余暇時間は菜園や森作りなど創造的な時間に生かしていました。こうしたやり方なら、郊外で相当広い土地を求めて、願いをかなえられるはずです。

　誰しも不本意な役回りに巡りあわないとも限りません。あるいはお金や、地位を守るために、ウソをついたり、公序良俗に反する役回りなど引き受けたりしたくないはずです。そのためにも身の程をわきまえ、この人生なら貧乏でも満足との生き方を見定め、覚悟を決め、いざというときに備えた不断の努力を傾けてはどううでしょうか。

　こうした考え方のもとに私は仕事に立ち向かい、伸び伸びと仕事に励みながら自活力を高める日々を過しています。また、人形作家を目指し、人形教室や喫茶店の経営を始めた妻を励ましています。裏返して言えば、給与など、自分がぶら下がっている糸が何らかの事情で切れたぐらいで、急に生活が成り立たなくなるような生き方を、自立しているとは見たくない。そう考えていたのがよかったように思います。

（産経新聞コラム「自活のススメ」20070112、
原題「本当の自立を目指す」）

7. 本当のソロバンをはじく （1999年6月21日）

　日差しが強くなると、いつも思い出すことがあります。それは5年前に、太陽光発電機の関西初の民間設置者となった時のことです。

　次々と取材を受けましたが、採算を度外視して設置した理由と、設置後の電力使用量の変化について、事実をなかなか理解してもらえなかったのです。

　当時は、機器が高くて国の補助金を得ても採算はまったく合いませんでした。「なのになぜ設置したのか」との詰問です。もう一点は、設置後の消費電力は「減ったはず」との思い込みを、なかなか解いてもらえなかったことです。

　太陽光発電機は従来の電力会社と売買契約を結んで設置します。発電しない夜間はそれまで通りに電力を買い、昼間は余剰電力がでると売って月末に清算するわけです。

　ですから記者は、設置後の電力使用量は減って当然と見たようで、「増えた」という私を疑ってかかったのです。現実に、後に続いた設置者は皆、家族ぐるみで節電に努力し、余剰電力の売上金を増やしていました。妻も私も電気の消し忘れなどもします

が、設置後はあまり節電に努めていません。ですから増えたに違いないと考えたわけです。しかし、信じてもらえなかっただけでなく「奥さんを呼んでほしい」と迫る記者までいました。

　経緯が分からないまま、妻は動き始めたビデオカメラの前に座らされ、同じ質問を受けました。「増えましたよ。だって、罪悪感がなくなりましたから」

　もう一点は、採算が合わない機器を設置した理由です。　思い余って次のように答えました。「わが家では、車は軽四輪、飼っている犬は雑種です。逆に、太陽光発電機は高くても欲しかった。それがわが家流の贅沢です」

　これらの回答はどの報道機関にも採用されませんでした。　もちろん、太陽光発電機が耐用年数内に生み出す総エネルギー量は、機械の生産、設置、あるいは廃棄などに要する総エネルギー量を上回っている、と聞いた上で設置しています。

（神戸新聞コラム「随想」19990621
「本当のソロバン」）

8. 価値を創造する （2005年12月16日）

　ホームステイの長女エリザベスは薪割りが得意でしたが、滞在中に陶芸を学び、5つの湯飲み茶碗を置き土産にしました。クモを怖がった次女のシャノンも、忘れ得ない贈り物のし方を私たちに気づかせました。

　百貨店のクリスマス商戦が始まった頃に、次女はミシンを貸してほしいといいだし、毎日のように縫い物をしたり、大きなリュックサックを背負って担当教官のお宅に出かけたりするようになりました。

　この次女は学費などを稼ぐために路上で物売りもしていました。アメリカから持ってきたアクセサリーを見せ、いくらなら買うかと尋ねたことがあります。アメリカでは写真のモデルをして稼いだこともあったようで、思い出の一枚を残して帰っています。

　シャノンが背負うリックサックはしだいに大きくなりました。わが家では端切れを生かしてやたらと大きなパッチワークに挑んでいました。

クリスマスイブに、彼女は大きな紙包みを持ち出してきて、私たちの前に差し出したのです。開いてみると、わが家で縫っていたものと色違いのホーム炬燵用の掛け布団が出てきました。早速その夜から幾年かにわたって愛用することになりました。

　長女エリザベスの残した湯飲み茶碗は大きさや重さが少しずつ異なりますが今も用いており、時々糸尻の側に入ったサインを眺めては懐かしんでいます。シャノンの残した掛け布団は今やほとんど用いていません。しかし、昨年の暮れに野外で来客と鍋を囲みましたが、その時は久しぶりに取り出し、見慣れた刺繡のサインを示し、ひとしきり話に花を咲かせました。質素で誠実な２人が残した暖かくて大きな贈り物です。

（産経新聞コラム「自活のススメ」20051216、
原題「心に残る贈り物」）

9. 相互扶助を心がける （2005年1月7日）

　皆さんはどのような元旦をお迎えでしたか。わが家では神棚にお灯明をあげ、仏壇の両親に新年の挨拶をした後、新婚間なしに揃えた正月用の什器で祝いました。お屠蘇を注ぎあって「今年もよろしくお願いします」などと挨拶を交し、梅昆布茶や雑煮をいただくわけです。その上で、妻が大晦日に準備したお煮しめや酢の物などのお節料理を噛み締めました。

　母が健在の時は、ボウダラとか黒豆の煮しめや数の子を漬け込むのは母の担当でしたが、今では同じ調理方法で妻が用意します。夕食にはハマグリの澄まし汁とか茶碗蒸しが加わりますが、他は朝夕とも同じで、お節料理を三が日の間に片付けます。昼食は、妻が喫茶店を年始のお客さまのために開けるようになってからは一人でとっています。餅好きの私は、醤油味の焼き餅を海苔で巻いてよく食します。

　三が日の雑煮は白味噌仕立てで、コイモ、人参、大根、ゴボウ、豆腐が入っています。その後は、青菜、かしわ、シイタケ、蒲鉾を使った汁に、焼いた丸餅を入れる澄まし雑煮が登場します。近年は好物の数の子やナマコが高くなったのが気に入りませんが、わが家の食文化を大切に守っています。

　家族の結ばれ方は様々でしょうが、わが家では家族が造った手料理を家族が揃ってとることをとても大切にしています。それが家族の心に自活の精神を育む根本のように見るからです。家族が心を一つにして助

け合い励まし合うことが、暮らしを豊かにする秘訣だと考えているわけです。

自己完結能力を高める根本は、相互扶助ではないでしょうか。今や妻は、小料理屋を開けそうな腕前です。今年も、こうした想いを新たにする元旦を迎えました。

（産経新聞コラム「自活のススメ」20050107、
原題「食文化を守る」）

10. 小さな巨人を目指そう （2006年7月7日）

短期大学の学長に選ばれたときのことを思い出しました。「環境保護」という大テーマを打ち出し、心を一つにしたことはすでに触れましたが、その一環として短大では珍しい総合的な学科編成であった点を生かしています。

デザイン美術科、音楽科、歯科衛生科、幼児教育科と、芸術系2科、医療系と教育系各1科という編成でした。ですから「『一隅を照らす』人になろう」と呼びかけ、たとえ小さくとも総合能力をわきまえた巨人のような人を育もうとしています。

たとえば、小さな歯科医院が採用してみたら、技能の優れた歯科衛生士であっただけでなく、カーテンの色柄やBGMがよくなり、グリーンも枯れなくなり、子どもがすぐになつくようになった、とあれば大歓迎されることでしょう。

ですから、学科の壁を取りはらう必要性を訴えただけでなく、デザイン美術科には「園芸療法」の講座を設けてもらい、音楽科には「音楽療法士」のコースを強化してもらうなど、学生が希望すれば総合的な能力を身に付け、生業にも挑戦しやすくしています。

当初は聴講生のような扱いしかできませんでしたが、いずれは単位まで与えられる学校にして、自己完結能力の向上に魅力を感じる若者をひきつける学校にしよう、と訴えたわけです。

近代は、人間を専業化分業化してロボットのように単能化し、互いに競わせる傾向にありました。それが各人の心を殺伐としたり自然の摂理に疎くさせたりしてしまい、環境破壊や家庭崩壊あるいは孤独化などにも結び付けていたように私は思います。だからたとえ一隅であれ、ほのぼのとした雰囲気をかもし出す小さな巨人を育みたかったのです。

（産経新聞コラム「自活のススメ」20060707、
原題「小さな巨人を目指す」）

11. 美意識や価値観を見直す （2006年9月29日）

中国はものすごい勢いで変化しています。1986年から時々訪ねてきましたが、訪ねる度に街や人々の生活がアメリカ化している、といってよさそうです。

この度は京都府立大学と雲南農業大学の合同シンポジュームがきっかけで、その会議の円卓につく機会も与えられました。中国政府は「農家楽」と呼ぶ少数民族を「観光」の目玉にする活動を推し進めていますが、学者は観光の域に留めず「交流」の域に、つまり対等の関係にまで高めようとしているようで、とても有意義なシンポジュームだ、と感じました。

私にも持論を展開する機会を与えられました。そこで、世界遺産を目指す「土戈塞村」、世界遺産になった日本の「白川郷」、そして

20　1章　AI時代に備える12のヒント

アメリカのアーミッシュの村々を対比しながら、キーワードで言えば「啓蒙」の空間にしてはどうか、と訴えました。これは、西洋から始まった工業文明が農業文明より高尚な文明とは考えず、工業社会は早晩破綻するに違いないとの見方から生まれた意見ですから容易に理解されるはずがありません。だが一石を投じておきたかった。

アーミッシュは総勢15万人ほどですが、宗教の教義に従って農業を基盤とした2百年来の自給自足生活を守っており、その集落は毎年何百万人もの観光客を惹き着けています。とりわけ大量消費生活や拝金主義に疑問や不安を抱き始めたアメリカ人が、その異なる価値観や美意識に触れて目を見張り、大いなる啓蒙を受けているように見受けられます。

中国の「農家楽」も、観光客に媚びるのではなく、持続可能な次の生き方を創出するヒントの宝庫として固有の文化に意義や価値を見出し、観光客の啓蒙に活かしてはどうでしょうか。

（産経新聞コラム「自活のススメ」20060929、
原題「観光より啓蒙を」）

12. 清豊を目指す（2005年5月20日）

「日本環境教育学会」の第16回大会が京都教育大学で始まっており、明日催されるシンポジュームでは「次の生き方」との演題で私が基調講演をさせてもらいます。

世界中の人が私たちのような生き方を真似たら、地球はたちまちパンクします。先進工業国の人口は2割に過ぎないのに、世界が毎年産出する資源の8割と食糧の5割を消費し、炭酸ガスの6割を排出するような生き方をしているからです。とはいえ、誰しも昔の生活には戻りたくないでしょうし「清貧」になるわけにも行かないでしょう。そこで、同学会は私に目を着けたようです。

演者の紹介文を見ますと、著書に『次の生き方　エコから始まる仕事と暮らし』（平凡社）があり、繊維産業の第一線に身を置く一方で、「清貧」ではなく「清豊」を旨とする「次の生き方」＝「自然ドロボウにならずに済ませられる生き方」を追及・実践してきた、とありました。

実はこの本に私は『清豊を求めて』という副題をつけようとしていました。当コラムでも清豊を求めるヒントを連載したいと願っています。それは、これまでの大量消費を競うような生き方は早晩消費税の増額や環境税などの創設を不可欠にするからです。

そうと気付いた人から順に、お互いに「個性の発揮を尊重しあう創造的な生き方に転換しましょう」と呼び掛け合いたいです。水や空気を汚したり石油や石炭を採掘し尽くしたりせずに、環境問題を自動的に解消しながら世界中のすべての人が心豊かになれる生き方があるのです。その第一歩は、既製品の大量消費を促すフロー型の生き方から、創造の喜びに満ち溢れたストック型の生き方へとまず意識を切り替えることではないでしょうか。

（産経新聞コラム「自活のススメ」20050520、
原題「清豊を求めて」）

Wisdom for the Era of Artificial Intelligence: 12 Lessons

1章

Lesson 1 Honor the Original

(Sankei News column: "In Favor of Self-sufficiency" August 19, 2005, Title: "Measure of Happiness")

Have you ever chastised yourself for buying something you shouldn't have or doing something you regretted? I used to do this on a regular basis, but in recent years I have learned to avoid this kind of thing by relying more on myself.

In the wake of these regrettable failures, I realized that there was a common thread among them. It was my sense of inferiority, exacerbated by a kind of anxiousness that made me bluster forward without exercising good judgment. In short, I did not have a set of personal standards and principles, thus making me vulnerable to manipulation by those around me.

I have been working on establishing my own principles and tenets, and making a clear and concerted effort to stick to them. However, so as not to be seen as an oddball, when I got married, I announced my thoughts to my wife.

"The measure of my happiness is the number of times I eat your home-cooked meals and the number of times I wear the dress shirts you have washed for me over the course

of our lives together."

In the same way a man often decides that his mother's cooking is the best in the world, I took pleasure in determining my idea of what the best in the world was. You can do this within the confines of your own home, so as to avoid clashing with others. Of course, I placed this burden on my wife, but eventually my wife's cooking and the amount of starch in the laundry she did for me became what I was most comfortable with.

Over the years, gradually those things I judged by my own criteria grew in scope and I was no longer satisfied with just fastidiously selecting items from among available products. I have come to make more and more things in a DIY mode, which has also required that I learn the mastery of a variety of tools. This gradually enhanced my self-sufficiency, and has allowed me to achieve a more distinctive way of life, indeed an original one.

This all served to solidify my own principles and thus dramatically reduced my worry and anxiety.

Lesson 2 Determining Principles

(Asahi News Column: "On Living" October 14, 1995, Title: "Bound by Green Land")

I was first employed in 1962. I had been in a quandary about where I should get a job. I could not decide whether I wanted to find one within commuting distance from the lush green rural area of my home, or face up to moving to another location. All the companies I was considering were in large metropolitan centers. This was during the time of Japan's rapid economic growth, and large cities were anything but green. On the con-

trary, places like Osaka held up smoke stacks as a point of pride and symbols of prosperity. Ultimately, I chose a trading company in Osaka to which I could commute to from my parents' house in Kyoto. In my interview I announced, "I understand that it is the company's prerogative to transfer me to another office at some point, but if it comes to that then it is my prerogative to quit." Despite this pronouncement, I was among the 200 new male employees hired that year.

The year after I was hired, with the help of the Housing Loan Corporation, I built a modest house a short distance away from my parents' home nestled in at the foot of a mountain. It is the home I live in today. I immersed myself in gardening and landscaping on the weekends.

I was grateful to my company, which allowed me to pursue this kind of "green" (gardening and landscaping) lifestyle, and in return I dedicated myself to my work as well. I think it is safe to say that I accomplished more than the average employee.

There has been much change in my life, but I find myself still living here today, never having lived anywhere else. The flip side of this is that my life could be considered one confined to lush greenness.

I have given some thought to why I am confined to "green." Perhaps it was my father's influence. My father, who was bedridden as a younger man, got me 20 chickens when I had just started elementary school, and goats when I got to middle school. This was his contribution to helping my mother who was trying to support the family through the farming she was still struggling to make a go of. Even as a child, I learned the importance of plants in our lives as it pertains to life's food chain. Those plant-eating animals were an important source of protein for us.

If you think about it, a lion consumes a deer which is an herbivore. Animals cannot live without the oxygen given off by plants. In essence, animals cannot lives without plant life. Since then I have not left this green environment, and have continued to practice organic gardening in which we fertilize the plants we grow with our own waste and kitchen garbage.

Perhaps there is a relationship between my green lifestyle and the color theory I studied in college. Even now I clearly remember what I was taught about the effect of the color green. When surrounded by green our pulse and blood pressure tend to decrease, our bodies excrete lower levels of hormones and we perceive the passage of time as more languid. Conversely, fast food restaurants and instant food packaging often use red and other bold, hot colors, which tend to elicit a sense of urgency or agitation.

Thinking back, it was good that I deliberated about what job I was going to take. It made me realize the importance of one's principles. Since then, I have prioritized green space, spending time in that space and a way of life I build with my own tools. I have distanced myself from that which is the opposite of this kind of life, and that has gradually enhanced my self-sufficiency. I can't help but feel that this allowed me to achieve a way of living that truly reflects who I am.

Lesson 3 Change Your Mind With Humility

(Gifu News Column: "General Outline" August 30, 2001, Title: "Changing One's Mind")

It was 56 years ago in 1962 when President Kennedy, faced with the life and death matter of the Cuban missile crisis, held a press conference and referred to one specific book he had read.

I had just been hired at a trading company that spring, and I envied of the massive scale of America where personal income was 5 times that of Japan, and car ownership was 25 times that of Japan. It motivated me to work even harder. It took about a quarter of a century for Japan to catch up, but in the process it appears that Japan has managed to over-

look one critical issue after another. One of the most conspicuous of these was this book that changed the world dramatically upon its publication.

There were many Japanese who were posted in America by the trading company I worked for. However, not one of my Japanese colleagues paid any particular attention to this book, which had aroused much controversy in the United States at that time. From my current standpoint, it is safe to say that even as we Japanese threw ourselves intently into the pursuit of profit and popular trends, we were impervious to the proposition this book proposed: a change in perspective.

My work at that time largely had to do with apparel and the fashion world, so I took an interest in the American clothing company, Gap, which introduced apparel targeted at all ages and genders, and came to stand for basic clothing for all Americans. In the subsequent 30 years since, it has become a one-trillion-yen company. The outdoor clothing company Patagonia revived its business as a vehicle to revolutionize society, and firmly determined its mission to be passing on a better world environment to the next generation. These are

businesses that provide the backdrop for the landscape in which we get furtive glimpses of the book which turned the tide of people's thoughts and times, and which became the shining classic of environmental issues: Rachel Carson's *Silent Spring*.

Japan is struggling with a sense of entrapment. I hope that first we will consider, with humility, Carson's proposition that we change our minds, and that we work on the specifics of turning the tides away from old conventional ways toward new currents. I encourage you to revisit this book as a first step in that direction.

Lesson 4 Teaching "Grit"

(Sankei News Column: "In Favor of Self-sufficiency", January 20, 2006, Title: "Responsibility and an Allowance")

Ricky, the son of a corporate executive I did business with in America, did not receive a monthly allowance. His parents passed on to him, an only child, the notion that money is remuneration for work. Ricky told me that when his parents were not at home, that was his chance to earn pocket money. His mother, for example, paid him for watering the plants and keeping them healthy.

Both parents and child reported that they had never heard of anyone else in the neighborhood who got an allowance just as a family right. Girls babysat, for example, and families and neighbors asked children to do odd jobs commensurate with their abilities. In this way the children were given appropriate responsibility and earned their own money.

One weekend I was invited to this family's house. Ricky was looking forward his father's return because he wanted to ask him if he

could wash the car, which he had done in the past. However, the father put the child's request aside, and instead told his son to come with him on an errand. I asked to go along with them in the car, as I wanted to see what the father had in mind.

Our destination was a gas station. The father had his car washed and made sure his young son saw him pay. The father had been paying his son the same amount as the price of a car wash.

On the way home, the father asked his son, "If you had to choose, Ricky, whom would you ask to wash your car?" He made his son compare the outcome of the gas station car wash and his. "Of course," added the father, "if the outcome is the same, then I would want to give you first crack at it." And then consistent with his upbringing, the son asked his father for another chance to wash the car properly.

Lesson 5 Enlarge Your Sphere of Responsibility

(Sankei News Column: "In Favor of Self-sufficiency", January 28, 2005, Title: "True Ability")

Japan is experiencing a decline in scholastic ability and an increase in incidents of medical errors, but can we solve the problem of medical errors by improving scholastic ability under the current education system?

In our home, we strive toward the ideal of

a spiritually fulsome life where we work hard to enhance our own self-sufficiency. The key to doing this is to improve one's own ability to assume responsibility and then broaden those parameters. There are some things in life, however, as with health care, where we have no choice but to rely upon the skills of a person of like mind, and face up to entrusting our life to them.

I lost both my parents in the past 10 years. Prior to their passing, both of them were cared for by our local general practitioner. At the outset, the practice of medicine is generally accompanied by errors and shortcomings, which can lead to serious remorse. Rather than prioritizing the newest medical devices and facilities or most advanced technology, my wife and I have favored physicians to whom we might extend compassion in the event that an error is made.

If the solution to this issue is a matter of character, then I remain dubious as to whether or not an improvement of scholastic ability that does not focus on improvement of character is the answer. There are detrimental effects to society when we treat human beings strictly by the book, see the human body as a collection of parts, and presume to judge character by standard test scores.

My father suffered from influenza which got continuously worse, and my mother had been in a small local hospital to be treated for colon cancer. Both, however, wanted the same thing: to die at home. Therefore we made up our minds to provide care for them as part of our family responsibilities, and we were supported by house calls from our doctors whom we considered of like mind. I feel confident that both my parents died in peace. I am most fortunate in that I parted with my parents without any unresolved issues.

Lesson 6 How Much is Enough?

(Sankei News Column: "In Favor of Self-sufficiency" January 12, 20007, Title: "Aim for Real Independence.")

When I was working as chief of staff in the president's office of a company in Kobe, many of the young employees there came to me around the time they were considering marriage to discuss low-interest home loans provided by the company. As long as they were going to make that large outlay of money, I urged them to purchase as much land as they could, and make their personal lives as rich as possible.

If one's personal life is fulfilling, it is possible to endure the demands of a workplace as long as the work itself is worthy. I encouraged these young people to determine their life goals early on, taking into consideration their and their spouse's character and personality. For example, if they had an affinity for making pottery, they should make long-term plans such as planting trees, which would eventually become fuel for firing a kiln.

During those years, I stayed in a small condo close to work on weekdays, and went back to my home base in Kyoto on weekends. I used my free time creatively, gardening and cultivating a grove of trees on my property. I

maintained that, if those young people took the same approach I did, they too would be able to realize their dreams by seeking a fairly large property in the suburbs.

There is no guarantee that you will not be assigned a role at work which you would rather not take on. No one wants to play a role that runs contrary to the greater good just for money's sake. Thus, we need to understand who we are, and determine the kind of life we will lead, even if it means living in poverty. With that resolve, we should work tirelessly in the event that we are faced with those circumstances.

I approach my work with this philosophy. I do my best to enhance my self-sufficiency while engaging in my work with both a sense of security and vitality. I also support and encourage my wife in her work as a doll artist. She teaches at her studio and runs a café as well. We are independent enough financially not to have our world come crashing down around us should the lifeline by which we find ourselves suspended suddenly breaks. I am content with this approach to life.

Lesson 7 A Real Abacus

(Kobe New Column: "Reflections" June 21, 1999, Title: "A Real Abacus")

I am reminded of one thing in particular every time the sun shines brightly: five years ago we became the first people in the Kansai region to have solar panels installed on a private residence.

We responded to multiple requests for interviews from the media, but it was difficult to get them to understand first, why we went ahead with solar panels without regard for any return on investment, and second, the difference in our electric bill after installation.

At that time, solar panels were very expensive and thus didn't make sense financially even with the support of government subsidies. The journalists persisted in interrogating us about why we installed solar panels despite all the deterrents. It was also hard to get them to let go of their predisposition that our consumption of electricity would decrease after installation.

When you install solar panels, you sign a contract with the electric company. You pay for the electricity used at night when the panels are not producing electricity, and sell the generated surplus back to them during the day. The electric bill is settled up at the end of the month.

The journalists took it for granted that our consumption of electricity would decrease. They doubted me when I told them otherwise. In reality, many families who install solar panels in their homes subsequently also make concerted efforts to save electricity, and are able to profit from the surplus electricity they sell back. My wife and I haven't really made any particular effort to save electricity, and in fact, we often forget to turn off the lights when we leave a room. So our actual consumption could only have increased. Not only did the journalists not believe me, they even demanded that I bring out my wife for questioning.

My wife appeared and was placed in front of a video camera. Without knowing what had already transpired, she was asked the same question about our electricity consumption, to which she replied, "Our consumption has increased. But you see, we don't feel guilty about it anymore."

The other point of contention was the financial impracticality of solar panels. Unable to contain myself any longer, I told them, "In our family we only own a Kei-car, and our dogs are mutts. But in this case, we wanted solar panels regardless of the cost. This is what we consider a true luxury in our home." None of these responses was published in any media outlet. Of course, we installed the panels knowing full well that the total energy output of the panels for their service life would exceed the total energy necessary to manufacture the devices, complete the installation and ultimate disposal.

Lesson 8 Create Value

(Sankei News Column: "In Favor of Self-sufficiency" December 16, 2003, Title: "Gifts for the Soul")

The first international student we hosted was Elizabeth, who was, incidentally, particularly good at chopping wood. During her time in Japan she studied pottery, and made five teacups, which she gave to us as a parting gift. Our second international student, Shannon (who was, incidentally, afraid of spiders) gave us an unforgettable example of gift giving.

Around the time department stores were starting their Christmas campaigns, she asked to borrow a sewing machine. First, she worked daily on an unnamed sewing project at our house, but then started going to her Japanese language teacher's house shouldering a big backpack.

This is the same young woman who sold things on the street in Japan to pay her tuition. She showed me some of the accessories she brought with her from the United States and asked me how much I would pay for them. She apparently worked as a model in America to earn money as well. She gave us one of her photos when she went home.

Shannon's backpack got gradually bigger and bigger. It turned out that she was making an enormous patchwork quilt using fabric remnants.

On Christmas Eve she brought out a huge package and placed it in front of us. Inside the package was the quilt she sewed at our house and a kotatsu quilt of the same design but in different colors, which she sewed at her teacher's house. We used the quilts from that evening on and have loved them over the course of many years.

The tea cups that our first international student, Elizabeth, gave to us are all slightly different in size and shape. I still use them and think nostalgically about her when I have occasion to look at the signature on the foot of the cups. We hardly use the quilt that Shannon gave us anymore. However, toward the end of last year when we had guests over for an outdoor hot-pot party, we brought the quilt out and showed off the embroidered signature on it. From there the conversation blossomed over the course of the evening. That was the warm great-hearted gift that those two naturally generous people left for us.

Lesson 9 Mindful of Mutual Support

(Sankei News Column: "In Favor of Self-sufficiency" January 7, 2005, Title: "Perpetuating Ritual Cuisine")

How did you spend your New Year's Day? At our house, after lighting a votive candle at the house shrine, we made New Year's supplications to my parents in front of our Buddhist altar. Then we celebrated using the familiar dishes and plates my wife and I acquired not long after we were married. We always pour ceremonial New Year's sake for each other and exchange ritual greetings asking for the goodwill and indulgence of the other for the coming year. Then we have *kelp-plum tea* and our customary *o-zoni*. On top of all this, we savor the *o-sechi* cuisine of simmered vegetables and vinaigretted dishes my wife prepares on New Year's eve.

When my mother was still alive, she was responsible for making dishes like the black bean dish called *bodara*, and the pickled herring roe; but now it is my wife who prepares these dishes following the same recipe. In the evening we have dishes such as clear clam soup and savory steamed egg custard, but all other meals are *o-sechi* cuisine, which we generally polish off over the course of the first three days of the year. Since my wife has taken to opening her café to customers at New Year's, I now have my New Year's Day lunch on my own. Being a *mochi* lover, I of- ten grill *mochi* seasoned with soy sauce and wrap it in

nori for lunch.

Our New Year's *o-zoni* is made with *white miso*, taro, carrots, *daikon*, burdock root and *tofu*. We also have a clear version of *o-zoni* with greens, chicken, *shiitake mushrooms* and *kamaboko*, and each serving includes a round, grilled *mochi*. I resent the fact that my favorite herring roe and sea cucumber have gotten so expensive recently, but we still keep them on the menu to honor the importance of ritual cuisine in our home.

Families are bound together in different ways, but in our home we place great impor-tance on gathering for a homemade meal. We see this as the foundation of the spirit of independence in the heart of the family. The secret to a fulfilling life is uniting the hearts of all family members, supporting and encouraging each other each in our separate endeavors.

Lesson 10 Little Giants

(Sankei News Column: "In Favor of Self-sufficiency" July 7, 2006, Title: "Become a Little Giant")

I have been reminiscing about when I was selected as the president of a junior college. I have already mentioned my efforts to unify that institution under the overarching theme of "environmental protection." As an exten-sion of that, I have capitalized on a compre-hensive curricular structure that is quite rare in a junior college.

This curriculum incorporates Design and Fine Arts, Music, Dental Hygiene, Early Childhood Education, which encompasses two Art courses, one Public Health, and one Education course. I urge everyone at the insti-tution to "light up a corner", and to nurture people who will realize their comprehensive abilities in a big way, no matter how modest the size of the college.

Here is an example of what I mean. Let's say a dental office hires a person who is a tech-nically skilled hygienist, and on top of that, let's say this all led to new curtains, better BGM, no more neglected dead plants, and children who are happy to be cared for by this hygienist. That dental office would benefit greatly from hiring someone like that. At this junior college, not only have I chal-lenged conventional academia to recognize the necessity of removing disciplinary par-titions, but I also had the Art Department offer supplemental courses in horticultural therapy, and had the Music Department of-fer courses in music therapy. This allows for acquisition of a broad set of skills, which, should a student desire it, and make it easier for them to find their vocation.

In the initial stages, students were only allowed to take these interdisciplinary classes as auditors, but eventually I got the college to allow them to receive credit. In short, I asked the school to become an institution that could attract young people who want to enhance their inherent multifaceted abilities. In recent years the general trend has been to focus on specialization with narrow skill sets, as if we were robots, and have pitted ourselves competitively against each other. In my opinion, this has led to inhumane be-havior, estranged us from the providence of nature, and even led to degradation of the environment, collapse of the family as well as isolation. Even if it is only one small corner, I want to encourage "little giants" who can provide warmth to the world in their own modest way.

Lesson 11 Rethinking Aesthetics and Values

(Sankei News Column: "In Favor of Self-sufficiency" September 29, 2006, Title: "Enlightenment over Tourism")

China is changing at an alarming rate. Since 1986, I have visited China several times, and I think it is fair to say that every time I go their cities and lifestyles have be-come more Americanized.

Recently, I was given the opportunity to join a round table discussion at the joint sym-posium of Kyoto Prefectural University and Yunnan Agricultural University. The Chinese government has been promoting ethnic mi-nority agricultural collectives as an object of tourism. Scholars, however, did not want to stop with mere tourism, but rather wanted to encourage exchange between tourists and the collectives from positions of equality. In my opinion, this was a very meaningful symposium.

I was also given the opportunity to present my own thinking at this gathering. I unpacked my thoughts on developing certain spaces as spaces of enlightenment, as I compared Tugozhai village, which aspires to be a World Heritage Cultural Site; Japan's Shirakawa-go, which is a World Heritage Cultural Site; and America's Amish culture. Each of these entities maintains that Western industrial civilization is not superior to agrarian civilization, and that industrial society will inevitably fail. This position is not one that everyone is going to catch on to immediately. But, regardless, I still wanted to throw

a pebble into the pond.

The Amish population is perhaps 150,000 strong, and they have perpetuated their self-sufficient agrarian lifestyle for 200 years in accordance with their religious beliefs. Their communities attract millions of tourists every year and I think this is because, in essence, Americans who have serious reservations about mass consumerism and the worship of money attempt to seek out a different value system and aesthetic. They derive considerable "enlightenment" from the Amish.

Rather than currying favor only with tourists, the Chinese agrarian communities should derive meaning and value from their traditional cultures as a treasure trove of wisdom, which create the next mode of sustainable living and also bring enlightenment to tourists as well.

Lesson 12 Noble Wealth

(Sankei News Column: "In Favor of Self-sufficiency" May 20, 2005, Title: "Seeking Noble Wealth")

The 16th annual conference of the "The Japanese Society of Environmental Education" has begun at Kyoto University of Education, and I have been asked to give the keynote address on "The Next Way of Living" on the opening day of the event.

If everyone on the planet lived in the same manner we do, the planet would fail. This is because the population of advanced countries accounts for no more than 20% of the world's population, but it consumes 80% of the world's annual resources, 50% of the world's food, and produces 60% of the world's carbon dioxide. That said, no one wants to return to a past lifestyle, nor would it work for everyone to endure even noble poverty. This is the climate in which the conference sought me out as a speaker.

My bio among the presenters at the conference revealed this. "Mr. Mori has published *The Next Way of Living: Life and Work Based on Ecological Practices*. He places himself on the front lines of the textile industry while practicing and promoting "the next way of

living" (noble abundance not noble poverty) which is equivalent to 'a life in which we can get by without robbing nature.'"

Actually, I had intended to entitle the book, "Seeking Noble Wealth." The life we have led so far of competitive mass consumption will eventually lead to such things as a higher consumption tax and introducing an environmental tax, as well.

I want to call to action those who have been inspired, each in their own time, to transition to a creative way of life where we mutually respect the achievement and the full scope of each person's individuality. There is a life in which all people on the planet can feel fully contented, naturally ameliorating environmental problems, without polluting the water or air, or extracting petroleum or fossil fuels. As an initial step in this direction, we must first change our attitudes to reflect a change from "flow" which encourages mass consumption of ready-made goods to "stock" which is rich with the joy of creation.

1章　准备迎接人工智能时代的 12 个启示

1　尊重独创性

为什么买了这些东西？为什么做了那样的事？谁都有过烦恼后悔的时候吧！我经常是这样。但是通过提高自活力，这些悔恨好像少多了。

回想起来带有反省和后悔的失败，就会发现它们之间有一些共同之处。有时被不安和自卑感所折磨，有时是虚张声势缺乏判断力所造成的。也就是没能明确自己衡量事物的尺子（判断基准）被周围所摆弄。

因此我决定看准自己的尺子和座标，习惯做事都按照这些，努力去理解事物的原理。但是也注意这些不应该让世界摇头不解。如果要成家立业的人，就应该注意以下事项。

"这辈子能吃几次妻子做的菜，穿几次她洗的衬衫。这些是我的幸福标准"。就像"母亲的拿手菜"令我们吃起来高兴。我们认为"这才是世界上最好吃的东西"是无需理由的。我觉得像这样的任意属于隐私的范围，所以不会受到社会的厌弃。当然给妻子带来不少负担，渐渐地她做饭的咸淡和洗衣浆糊的多少都变得是我最适宜的。

慢慢地衡量对象多起来了。开始不能满足选择既成品的生活，驱使工具手工制作的频率高起来。这些逐渐提高了自活力，让我明确了人生的道路，也就是得到了富有个性的生活。同时，这些使自己的衡量标准和座标更加准确，烦恼也就少多了。

（产经报专栏"推荐自给自足"2005年8月19日
"幸福的标准"）

2　要看清原理

1962年我进入社会，但是决定就职的时候非常犹豫。是在自然丰富的田园地带可以通勤的范围内找，还是做好搬家的准备，不能马上决定。几个作为候选的就职地点都在大城市。当时正是高度经济成长期刚刚开始的时候，大都市没有绿色的自然，大阪等地被誉为"烟都"，成为繁荣的象征。

结果，我选择了从京都的家可以通勤的大阪的综合商社。所以在面试的时候我提出"如果公司突然下命令让我调动工作，我也许会突然辞职。"即使这样，新录取的男职员200多人里也有我一个。

进入公司的第二年，我在比父母家更远的山脚下，利用住宅金融公库贷款建了一个小小的家园，也就是现在的住所。开始了周末埋头干农活的日子。我感谢公司让我有一个在自然中生活的环境，努力工作，在工作上从不比别人差。

那以后虽然发生了各种各样的事情，但是没有离开过这个住处，一直到现在。反过来说，是这片富饶美丽的土地拴住了我的一生。

为什么土地会把我拴住？这让我深思。现在我想是因为亡父对我的影响吧。病床上的父亲为了帮助不习惯做农活还拼命支撑一家人生活的母亲，让我上了小学就开始养20只鸡，到了中学又开始养山羊。这些成为一家人维持生命的可贵的营养来源。虽然我是孩子，但是也学到怎样珍惜动植物。

此后，我一直没有离开过这片土地，用一家的粪便和食物垃圾来做肥料，坚持维护庭院的工作。

可能是因为在大学学习色彩论，关于绿色效果的知识现在还记忆深刻。在我们身边如果有绿色的话，心拍数和血压会下降，荷尔

蒙的排出量减少，感到时间过得缓慢。相反，快餐店以及即席食品的包装等为了催促购买欲或让人的情绪兴奋，所以多使用红色或橙色等暖色来达到效果。

现在回想起来，就职时的犹豫不是没有道理。让我知道了原理（原则）的重要性。那

之后我一直生活在自然丰富的绿色空间和时间里，并且优先工具。同时远远离开与这些相反的生活。这样逐渐提高了自活力，得到了符合自己的生活。

（朝日报专栏"生活考察"1995年10月14日
原题"绿色土地束缚了我"）

3 谦虚地转换思想

1962年（从现在算起56年以前）的今天，肯尼迪总统对古巴危机关系到国家存亡的问题，在记者招待会上曾经提到他刚读完一本著作，明确了一个指示。

那年春天在综合商社上班的我工作很努力，因为非常羡慕各方面都超过日本的美国，他们个人收入是日本的5倍，汽车普及率达到日本的25倍。那以后的日本用了25年的时间追上来，但是却将紧关重要的东西一个个地错过。其中显著的一个就是后来将世界改变的这部著作。

我工作的商社有很多美国驻员。我的工作有关服装，广泛地涉及时装行业。但是，当时在美国争论极大的这部著作却没有一个人表示关心。现在回想起来可以说，我们一味想着追求眼前的利益，对转换思想的建议是极其钝感的。

在那以后的美国，GAP公司推出以男女老少为对象的服装，后来又以"美国标准服饰"为标榜，创业30年就成长为一兆日元的企业。户外运动服的厂家巴塔哥尼亚公司作为改革社会的工具使企业再生，企业的使命是将更好的地球环境交给下一代继承。从这些动向的背景可以隐约看到蕾切尔·卡逊的《寂静的春天》，是这部著作使人们的意识和时代的潮流有所改变，作为环境问题的古典流芳百世。

现在的日本充满了封闭感。我希望首先应该谦虚地对待转换思想的建议，努力去除陈旧意识，寻找新潮流的所在。那么我们马上能做的就是重读这部著作。

（岐阜报专栏"素描"2001年8月30日
原题"意识的转换"）

4 注重交流 培养气概

在美国和我有过贸易来往的一个企业干部家里，每个月不给儿子瑞奇零花钱。他们的独生子要以自己的劳动才能换取父母的经济支援。

瑞奇告诉我，父母不在家的时候，"看家是挣钱的好机会"。比如给花盆里的植物浇水，不要让它们枯萎。母亲会按日子算给儿子工钱。

听他们父子讲，周围的邻居没有听说过，只凭父子关系就能得到每月的零花钱这样的道理。女孩子有的去做保姆，孩子们凭自己的能力打工，父母和孩子以及邻居之间相互商谈交易，然后让他们负责去做各种工作。

有一次周末接受邀请去干部家里做客。

瑞奇等着爸爸回来，像平时一样向爸爸提出"让我给您洗车吧！"但是父亲没有接受这个请求，而是当场要带儿子出去开车兜风。我也提出要一起去，因为我想知道父亲要对儿子做什么？

他们去的地方是加油站。父亲让加油站的人为他洗车，还让儿子看他是怎样支付洗车费的。原来父亲给儿子的洗车费和在加油站支付的钱数是完全同价的。

回家的路上，父亲问儿子："瑞奇如果是你的话，会让谁洗车呢？"这次父亲让儿子亲眼比较了一下加油站洗的车和瑞奇自己洗的

1章 准备迎接人工智能时代的 12 个启示 31

车有什么不同？如果站在选择的立场会怎么做？当然，父亲还加了一句："如果瑞奇和加油站洗得都很好，我会优先让你洗的。"儿子立刻请求："爸爸，再给我一次机会吧！"

（产经报专栏"推荐自给自足"2006年1月20日原题"责任感和零花钱"）

5　扩大自我责任的范围

现在社会上学力降低的问题和医疗失误的事件频发，如果以现今的方式提高学力是否可以解除医疗失误的问题呢？

我家向往精神丰富的生活，努力提高自给自足的能力。这些也提高了自己的负责感，并且扩大它的范围。

至于医疗，不管怎样总要麻烦他人，也就是说需要看好对方，做好将自己的生命托付给他人的思想准备，以坦然的态度去对待。

在这10年里我的父母都去世了，他们看病都是去街道熟悉的小诊所。医疗本身就容易发生失误和技术不足的问题，这些都会成为极其后悔的原因。所以我们夫妻俩的优先顺序不是最新的医疗设备等，而是可以信赖谅解的医生。即使在治疗上万一失策，我们反倒会体谅他"让大夫费心了"。

这是人品上的问题。目前学校在提高学力，却没有在磨练人品方面下工夫，所以看起来让人感到不安。对待人像按照说明书似的千篇一律，将人体看作用零件聚集起来的机器，用偏差值来衡量人格是否优秀，也许这些都是社会风潮所造成的弊病吧。

不光因流感严重去世的父亲，就连因大肠癌住进小医院的母亲，最后他们都希望回家在自己床上疗养。在家里请自己信赖的诊所医生或院长来出诊，家里人做好精神准备担负起照顾病人的责任。我想父母一定是放心咽气走的。我们对此分别没有任何遗憾。

（产经报专栏"推荐自给自足"2005年1月28日原题"真正的学力是什么？"）

6　知足者常乐

我在神户一所中坚企业做经理助理的时候，准备结婚的很多年轻人为了利用公司的低利息住宅贷款制度而来找我。每遇到这种情况我都向他们提议："一样用很多钱的话，还是尽量买片大点的土地努力充实私生活吧！"

私生活得到充实，就是工作辛苦些，我觉得如果是有益于健康的任务一定会坚持到底。所以我建议年轻人早期制定人生目标，好好考虑是否适合配偶者和自己的性格。比如喜欢陶艺的人就应该种植树苗，早点准备将来烤炉需要的燃料。

当时我在公司附近借了一间小小的公寓，平时住在那里。等到了周末就回京都私生活的据点，将休假日的时间都利用在种菜园和开辟森林等具有创造性的劳动上。如果按照这个做法，在郊外谋求相当广阔的土地就一定能达到自己的愿望。

我想谁都有可能运气不好，被迫做不情愿的工作。或者为了挣钱，接受自己不愿做的差事而违及公共秩序和良好风俗。因此我们需要识别分寸，这种人生即使贫穷也能满足。让我们看准生活方式，做好思想准备。建议大家预防万一，不断努力吧。

以这种思想为基础，我每天努力工作，活跃在岗位上，并且不断提高自活力。此外，妻子以人偶作家为目标，开始了人偶教室和咖啡店的经营。我鼓励妻子这样做，反过来说工资等自己挂在胸前的救命绳子也许会在什么时候被弄断。如果绳子因为什么理由被弄断，一下子不能生活的话，这种人生就不能算自立的生活。我能早期考虑到这些真是很幸运。

（产经报专栏"推荐自给自足"2007年1月12日原题"目标是真正的自立"）

7 打真正的算盘

阳光充足的时候我总会想起一件事。那就是5年前我成为关西地区第一个民间设置太阳能发电机的人。

接受接连不断的采访，因为设置这个把收支的核算置之度外，设置后电力使用量的变化等原因，都是记者们难以理解的事实。

当时机器价格很高，即使得到国家的补助金在核算上也亏本。记者们追问："知道不合算为什么还设置？"还有一点，他们以为设置后消费的电力一定会"减少"事实让他们不可思议。

太阳能发电机的设置是和以前使用的电力公司签订买卖契约。夜间不能发电就使用电力公司供给的电力，白天剩余的电力可以卖给电力公司，到了月末结算。

所以记者们认为设置后的电力使用量一定会减少，可是"增加了"的事实让他们怀疑。实际在我以后设置的人家都努力全家节电，使剩余电力的贩卖金额涨了上去。可是

我和妻子不但有时忘了关灯，设置后并不努力省电。所以我觉得一定增加了，可是他们不信，有的记者说："叫您爱人来核实一下吧！"

不知道原由的妻子被安排坐在开始转动的摄像机前，回答同一问题。妻子说："增加了！因为现在用电没有罪恶感。"

还有一点，为什么设置不合算的机器？我不知怎么解释才好，就说："我家只有一辆小汽车，一只杂种犬。所以太阳能发电机即使贵也买了。对我家来说它是唯一的奢侈品。"

我们的这些回答哪个报社都没有采用。当然，在设置太阳能发电机的时候知道它在耐用年数内生产的总能量超过机械的生产、设置、以及废弃等需要的成本。

（神户报专栏"随想"1999年6月21日
"打真正的算盘"）

8 创造的价值

留学住在我家里的伊丽莎白（我们把她当作长女）很会劈柴。在那段时间里她学了陶艺，做了五个茶杯留作纪念。另一个住在我家的留学生香农（我们把她当作次女）留下的礼物，方式同样让我们非常难忘。

百货店开始搞圣诞节促销的季节，次女说想借我家的缝纫机，此后每天都在缝纫什么东西，背个大背包出入于她的指导教师家里。

这个次女为了自己赚学费在路上摆摊卖东西。她把从美国带来的装饰品拿给我看，还问我如果多少钱想买？听说她还在美国打工做过摄影模特，回国的时候把她的照片留一张给我们留作纪念。

香农背的背包越来越大。在我家里试着

利用碎布做一个特大的拼布。到了圣夜她拿出一个很大的纸包，放在我们面前。打开一看，是一个和在我家做的不同颜色的桌炉被子。从那天晚上开始，这个被子我们一直珍惜用了好几年。

长女伊丽莎白给我们流下的茶杯大小和重量都不同，至今还在用。有时看着她在杯底写的名字觉得很亲切。香农留下的被子现在已经不太用了，但是去年年末在野外和来客一起吃火锅的时候把好久没用的被子拿出来，上边绣的名字那么眼熟，把它拿给客人看，这个话题说了好半天呢！两个人朴素诚恳，给我们留下了温暖又宝贵的礼物。

（产经报专栏"推荐自给自足"2005年12月16日
原题"难忘的礼物"）

9　注意相互扶助

大家是怎样迎接元旦的？我家在供神的架上点灯火，向供在佛坛的父母问候新年。然后用新婚后备好的新年餐具来庆祝。倒好屠苏相互说一些寒暄话："今年也请多多关照！"再喝酸梅海带茶，吃午饭烩年糕。此外还要品尝妻子除夕准备的煮菜和醋拌凉菜。

母亲健在的时候，过年是她负责做鳕鱼棒和煮黑豆还有酱鱼籽等，现在妻子用同样的做法准备年饭。除夕的晚饭加上蛤蜊清汤和鸡蛋羹，其他日子早晚都吃一样的菜肴。年饭一般在三天之内吃完。以后午饭的时间我一个人吃，因为妻子要开咖啡店迎接新年的客人。我非常喜欢吃年糕，烤好的年糕涂上酱油再用紫菜卷着吃很香。

我家的年饭前三天的烩年糕使用白酱，里面放小芋头、胡萝卜、大萝卜、牛蒡、豆腐。以后的烩年糕开始在清汤里放青菜、槲树叶、香菇、鱼糕蒲鉾、烤圆形年糕。可惜近年来我喜欢吃的干青鱼籽和海参都越来越贵，可是家里还是一直保持新年的饮食文化。

千家万户连结各自家庭的纽带各有不同，在我家里重视全家一起享受家庭菜的温馨和美味。认为这些是可以让家人心里培养起自给自足精神的根本。我觉得全家人能够同心协力，相互帮助和互相勉励才是生活得幸福充实的秘诀。

完全提高自己能力的根本是相互扶助。现在我的妻子做菜的手艺都可以开一家小饭馆了。今年我怀着这些想法迎接了崭新的元旦。

（产经报专栏"推荐自给自足"2005年1月7日
原题"维护饮食文化"）

10　做个小巨人

我想起被选为短期大学校长时的一些事。提出"环境保护"这个大主题，把师生的心连结起来是以前也提过的。作为其中的一个环节，编成综合学科充分利用，这在大专是非常少见的。

综合学科分为设计美术系、音乐系、齿科卫生系、幼儿教育系、艺术系2科、医疗系和教育系。呼吁学生"要做照亮角落的人"，培养学生即使身材渺小也要做具有综合能力的巨人。

比如一家小的牙科医院录取了一个技能高超的齿科护士。不但在工作上非常能干，就连医院窗帘的图案以及BGM也好多了。观叶植物不再枯萎，孩子们很快就和她熟起来了，大家对她的表现十分满意。

所以我提出废除学科之间的阻碍性，还在设计美术系设了"园艺疗法"的讲座。充实了音乐系"音乐疗法士"的课程。只要学生想学习就更容易培养她们的综合能力，积极向职业挑战。

我所提出的是，当初只能按照和旁听生同等待遇的学生，以后学校应该做到能给她们学分，提高完美自己的能力，吸引以此为荣的年轻人。

近代的倾向是将人专业化和分工化，像机器人一样简单化，然后竞争不相上下。我

认为是这些讨伐人心，让孩子们远离自然摄理，导致破坏环境，家庭瓦解。所以希望学生"要做照亮角落的人"培养带有和谐氛围

11　重新树立审美观和价值观

中国的变化速度惊人。从1986年几次访问，每次在街上看到的人们的生活好像都在美国化。

这次有幸参加京都府立大学和云南农业大学的合作主题讨论会，得到和专家们同桌交流的好机会。中国政府把称作"农家乐"的少数民族作为"观光招牌"极力推动此活动。学者们认为活动不只限于观光领域，应该宽展到"交流的领域"。也就是建立提高对等的关系。我感到这次主题讨论会开得非常有意义。

而且，在讨论会上我也有机会展开自己的论点。在此我将申请世界遗产的"土戈塞村"，已经成为世界遗产的"白川乡"，还有美国阿米什的村落相比较，讲述中的关键词是"启蒙的空间"。这个想法是不把西洋发起的工业文明看作高于农业文明，认为工

的小巨人。

（产经报专栏"推荐自给自足"2006年7月7日
原题"做个小巨人"）

业社会早晚一定会垮台。当然这个意见不会轻易地被接受，但是做到"水中投石"也是很有意义的。

阿米什人的总数不过15万人，他们遵守宗教的教义，以农业为生活基础，2百年来守护村落自给自足的生活。他们这些村落每年吸引几百万人的观光游客。特别是过着大量消费的生活和对拜金主义抱有疑问和不安的美国人，面对阿米什人不同的价值观和审美观都惊叹不已，好像受到了很大的启蒙。

我希望中国的"农家乐"也不要去迎合观光游客。而是作为智慧宝库，创造可以持续的崭新的人生。从固有文化中发现意义和价值，去启蒙观光游客。

（产经报专栏"推荐自给自足"2006年9月29日
原题"比观光更重要的是启蒙"）

12　以"清丰"为目标

"日本环境教育学会"的第16次大会在京都教育大学正式开幕，在明天召开的主题讨论会上我将做特邀报告。讲演题目是"崭新的人生"。

全世界的人如果都模仿我们的生活方式，地球立刻就要爆炸。先进工业国家的人口不超过全球的20%，但是把这些人的生活方式换算一下，每年消耗世界产出资源的80%，粮食50%，排出的废气占60%。虽然这么说，但是没有谁想回到过去的生活，更不想过"清贫"的生活。我的这些想法引起同窗会的注目。

讲演人的介绍是这样写的："《崭新的人生-以环保为基础的工作和生活-》（平凡出版社）的作者不但活跃于纤维产业的第一线，而且以清丰（不是清贫）为主旨，追求实践崭新的人生（不需要做自然强盗的生活

方式）"。

实际这本书的书名开始想以《追求清丰的生活》为题。这个专栏也想连载追求清丰的启示。因为至今竞争大量消费的生活早晚会导致消费税的增税和设立环境税等不可缺少的措施。

那么就让觉醒的人首先相互呼吁："让我们尊重个性，向富有创造的生活转换吧！"不要污染水源和空气，不要采掘用尽石油和煤炭，积极地解决环境问题，全世界的人都可以拥有精神充实的生活。实现它的第一步是改变生活方式，从促使大量消费既成品的流通型，转换到充满创造喜悦的储存型。首先让我们改换一下自己的意识吧！

（产经报专栏"推荐自给自足"2005年5月30日
原题"追求清丰的生活"）

2章 未来が微笑みかける生き方

　工業文明圏で暮らす私たちは、これからどのような国や人生を目指せばよいのでしょうか。そのありようが地球上の生きとし生けるものすべての命運を担っているように私は見ています。

　エコロジカルフットプリントの考え方に従えば、世界中のすべての人が今のアメリカ人並みの生き方を真似るには地球が5つ、日本人並みなら3つほど必要になります。私たちは1つの地球で生きていますから、工業文明人の生き方は地球に無理を強いているわけです。現実に、2017年のアース・オーバーシュート・デーは8月2日でした。つまり、地球上の植物が1年間に生み出す再生可能資源を、人類はこの日までに消費し尽くした計算です。利子だけで生計を成り立たせている人に例えていえば、1年分の利子をこの日までに使いつくし、8月3日以降は元本に手を付けていたことになります。ちなみに2018年は8月1日にと、この日は年々早まっています。

　拙著『次の生き方』を著したのは2004年ですが、工業文明圏の人口は11億人でした。その地球人口の2割が、（先に触れたように）地球が毎年生み出す地下資源やエネルギーの8割と食料の5割を消費していました。他方、人口13億人に達していた中国人が工業文明圏入りを急いでいる、と問題視しています。実は、こうした事態を予測し、備えたような生き方を私は若くして始めていたのです。

　そういう私も、もちろん当初は意識と身体は分離しており、矛盾した生き方をしていました。意識は工業デザインを学ばせ、総合商社に就職してファッションビジネスに関わり、欧米に足しげく通わせています。他方身体は、週末には郊外の自宅に戻り、元本を増やすような生活に勤しんでいたのです。それは、太陽と大地と雨を銀行のように見て、自分たちの生活が出すすべての有機物を定期預金のごとくに大地に返し、利子のごとくに野菜、果物、あるいは樹木などを育て、その範囲内で生きようと願い、土地を肥やし、樹木を太らせる生き方です。そしてこのストック型の生き方が、やがて人間にとってふさわしい生き方だと気付かされ、目覚めたのです。

なぜなら、工業文明人の生き方は、あらゆる動物が共有する「欲望の解放」を願っていたことに気付かされたからです。この気づきは、「清貧」に向かわせるのではなく、「人間の解放」を私に願わせるようになり、妻は創作料理に始まり人形創作に、私は日曜大工や菜園に始まり著作活動に勤しみ始めさせたのです。それを「清豊」と見たのです。

　この間に日本は、自動車や弱電気製品などを輸出して、その代金で生存する上で不可欠の食料や石油などエネルギー源を輸入する国になり、これらの自給率を落していました。とても脆弱で危なかしい国だと気付きました。

　その目で日本の歴史を振り返り、江戸時代の見方を変えました。300年近くにわたって鎖国をし、人口は3000万人に留まっていましたが、あらゆる人を創造的な生き方に誘い、経済成長していたのです。さらに歴史をくわしく見てゆくと、日本はその昔、多くの文物や思想などを中国大陸や朝鮮半島などから導入していました。

　その中国は、かつて世界有数の古代農業文明を誇っていましたが、他の古代農業文明と同様に豊かな森林を砂漠にしながら崩壊しています。現在、人口ではアメリカをはるかにしのぐ中国は、近代工業文明を謳歌しつつあり、アメリカ人のような生き方を目指しているかのように見えます。早晩これは、人類だけでなく生きとし生けるものを窮地に追い込みかねません。しかもこの生き方が、人間を真の豊かさや幸せに誘うのか、大いなる疑問が残ります。

　ここらあたりで人類は、「未来が微笑みかける生き方」に移行しなければならないのです。それは、世界中のすべての人が真似たら地球環境を復元しながら「人間の解放」を促す生き方です。それだけに、この冊子の翻訳を、留学生として1年間わが家で過ごしたエリザベスL.アームストロング先生と、『次の生き方』に共感いただけたことが契機で知り合えた劉穎先生に引き受けていただき、3か国語で完成させられたことを私はとても悦んでいます。

2章 Life the Future Smiles Upon

What kind of nation and way of life should we, the inhabitants of industrial civilizations, aspire to in the future? The fate of all living things on Earth depends upon this.

In terms of an ecological footprint, it would take about five Earths for everyone on the planet to live lives comparable to Americans, and approximately three Earths to live lives comparable to Japanese. All of us living on this planet as members of an industrial civilization are overtaxing the Earth. August 2, 2017 was "Earth Overshoot Day." This day marked when we maxed out a year's worth of Earth's natural resources. If this were a person living on investment income, they would have used up a whole year's worth of income by that day, and would have to begin drawing on their principle from August 3 on. Actually, the date was August 1 in 2018, and this date has been coming sooner and sooner each year.

I wrote *The Next Way of Life* in 2004 when the population of the industrialized world was 1.1 billion. 20% of the world's population, as I mentioned earlier, consumes 80% of the world's natural resources annually, and 50% of the world's food. I see the next problem arising in China, whose population has reached 1.3 billion and which is rapidly becoming increasingly more industrialized. I predicted these developments and I started living a life early on which prepared me for that eventuality.

Of course, in those years there was a contradiction between my focus at work and my personal convictions. In terms of the former, I studied industrial design, was involved in fashion at a large trading company, and traveled frequently to Europe and North America. The latter, on the other hand, had me returning to my home daily in the distant suburbs of Kyoto and dedicating myself to a lifestyle which reinforced my environmental principles. I consider the sun, the earth and the rain to be banks to which we return all organic matter generated from our daily lives, conserving as if we were putting money in a savings account. We grow vegetables, fruit, trees and shrubs the fruits of which are something akin to investment income. We aspire to live within those limits, cultivating the land and enhancing plant life. We woke up to that fact that this "stock" way of life is the most fitting for human beings.

I realized that life in an industrial civilization hopes for "liberation from desire" shared by all living beings. This realization in due course steered me not toward noble poverty, but rather "liberation for humanity." This is what inspired my wife to begin creative cuisine, and then her creative doll-making work, and me to begin DIY work, gardening and writing. This is noble wealth.

Over time Japan has become a country which exports various products such as cars and light electrical appliances, and with that income imports indispensable commodities and natural resources such as food and petroleum. This has reduced Japan's self-sufficiency. I have come to realize just how fragile and endangered Japan has become as a country.

Looking back into Japan's history with this in mind, my perspective on the Edo period has changed. Japan was in seclusion for nearly 300 years, during which time the population held at about 30,000,000, and the country drew everyone toward a creative way of living, which commensurately led to economic growth. A closer examination reveals that Japan imported much literature and philosophy from China and Korea.

China was formerly renowned for being the world's preeminent agricultural civilization of antiquity, but now it is being destroyed, with rich forests turning into deserts, a fate similar to other ancient agrarian civilizations. China, whose population far exceeds that of the United States, praises modern industrial civilization, and appears to be aspiring to a way of life comparable to the United States. Eventually, human beings and indeed all living things will be faced with a dilemma. Will this way of living lead to true wealth and happiness? I remain doubtful.

At this juncture the human race must move toward "life that the future smiles upon." That life is one, which, if the global community stands shoulder to shoulder, encourages "liberation for humanity" while restoring the Earth's environment. With this in mind, I am delighted that this modest publication is now available in English and Chinese thanks to the translators Elizabeth Armstrong, who spent a year living with us as a homestay student, and Liu Ying, whom I got to know as a kindred spirit after she read *The Next Way of Life*.

2章　未来向我们微笑的人生

生活在工业文明区域的人们今后想构建一个什么样的国家和人生，这关系到生存在地球的所有生物的命运。

根据生态足迹的想法来看，如果全世界的人都模仿美国人的生活，就需要5个地球。模仿日本人的话，也需要3个地球才够。但是话说回来，我们只能生活在1个地球。是工业文明的生活给地球带来巨大的负担。实际今年8月2日就是地球生态的超载日（人类消费的自然资源超过地球一年再生的资源产量和CO_2吸收量的日子）这个计算也就是说，人类将地球上的生物1年产出的再生可能资源在这个日子就已经耗尽。再打个比方，这和靠吃利息生活的人将1年的利息在这一天花光，8月3日以后的花费需要使用存款一样。而且这个地球过冲日变得一年比一年短，2018年是8月1日。

我在2004年出版的《崭新的人生》里提到，在工业文明圈生活的人口有11亿，仅占地球人口的20％。但是他们消费地球每年产出的地下资源和能源的80％，食物50％。问题是拥有13亿人口的中国也在赶紧加入工业文明圈。我从年轻的时候就开始过与这些消费无关的生活，仿佛预测到以后将要发生的事态。

当然最初意识与实际行动是分开的，我的生活方式曾经存在矛盾。意识让我学习工业设计，就职于综合商社，然后从事服饰贸易，经常去欧米出差。相反自己每到周末都要回到郊外的家，度过辛勤耕耘丰富原本的生活。也就是说，把太阳和大地的雨水当作银行，将自家生活中产生的有机物作为定期存款还给大地，培育的蔬菜、水果或者树木就像利息。我们希望在这个范围内生活，滋养土地和培育大树是我们人生中必不可少的。我们觉察到这种生活对人类来说是最好不过的了。

因为我发现在工业文明中生活的人，希望从所有动物共有的欲望中解放出来。这个觉察不但没有使我走向清贫，自然使我希望"解放人类"。于是妻子开始亲手制作菜肴和人偶，我也开始周末做木匠和开辟菜园，并且废寝忘食地写作。我们把这些看作"清丰"。

在此之间，日本出口汽车和家庭电器制品等，用这些获得的利益进口食品和石油等生存上不可缺少的物资。自给率的下降，让我感到这个国家变成依赖他国的脆弱而且危险的国家。

以此视点来回顾日本的历史，对江户时代的看法会有所变化。这个时代将近300年处于锁国（江户政府禁止基督教进入日本，也不允许日本人出境和入境。并且严格管理统治和限制贸易的对外政策），人口虽然只有3000万，但是诱导了人们发挥创意的生活，促进了经济成长。我们再仔细回顾一下历史，就知道日本以前的很多文物和思想等都是从中国大陆或者经过朝鲜半岛传来的。

中国过去以拥有世界屈指可数的古代农业文明而自豪，但是后来和其他古代农业文明一样使富饶的森林渐渐变成沙漠而走上崩溃之路。现在人口远远超过美国的中国讴歌着近代工业文明，生活模式看起来也好像也是以美国为模范。早晚这种生活不只人类，就连生物也会被逼入困境。而且，这种人生能不能带来真正的富有和幸福？是个很大的疑问。

到此地步，人类必须转换到 "未来向我们微笑的人生"。如果大家模仿去实行的话，那样就可以将地球的环境复原，促使"解放人类"。因此这本书的翻译具有很大的意义，以前留学日本在我家住过一年的伊丽莎白女士和赞同《崭新的人生》的刘颖女士能够接下这本书的翻译工作，现在将这本三国语言版本的书完成，我对此感到十分喜悦。

緑陰のアイトワ
aightowa in the verdant summer
绿荫里的爱永远农园

「アイトワ12節」 ～同じ心と出会うまで～
Twelve Views of aightowa: Encounters with those of like mind
爱永远农园12景～找到志同道合的伴侣～

この庭は、お金持ちだから造れた庭だと思う人がいるが、それは大違いだ。
この庭を創ったおかげで、私は豊かさを手に入れることができた。

There are those who assume that this garden was created by wealth.
That could not be farther from the truth.
We are blessed with richness and abundance thanks to this garden.

有人说:"这样的农园是有钱人才能建成的" 实际不是!
恰恰相反，是因为建了这个农园，我才真正富有起来。

スプートニクの打ち上げ
病気と受験の失敗で落胆する私

1957年、19歳。ソ連が打ち上げた人類初の人工衛星が飛んだ年。私は結核が治らず、大学受験に失敗。おそらく人生で最も落ち込んだ時期。いかに生きるべきかを突き詰めて考えた末に、母が耕作放棄したこの土地で自活することを覚悟した。

Sputnik launched.
Sick and failing, I became despondent.

It was 1957 and I was 19 years old. It was the year the Soviets launched Sputnik 1, the first man-made satellite. Unable to recover from tuberculosis, I failed my college entrance exams. It was perhaps the darkest moment of my life. After much thought, I resigned myself to living on this plot of land which my mother had let go fallow.

发射人工卫星
因疾病和高考失败而沮丧

1957年，我19岁。这一年苏联成功发射人类第一颗人工卫星。我的肺结核久久不愈，又加上高考失败。所以那时候可以说是人生最沉沦的时期，不得不翻来覆去地考虑今后自己怎么生存的问题。最后决定将母亲放弃耕耘的土地用来维生。

第2節 太陽が鼓舞した自立の夢

私が思い描いた生き方は、太陽の恵み、雨、この土地、そしてこの土地柄を活かすこと、であった。それは生態系を尊重し、動植物の生産力と自分たちが出すあらゆる有機物を活かす生き方だ。これが、私だけでなくすべての人の生きる根本であるはず、と思っている。

Second View Dream of self-sufficiency inspired by the sun.

The life I envisioned was one which made the most of the sun, the rain, and the inherent characteristics of the land. It was a life which put to good use the productivity of plants and animals and all the organic matter we generate, while honoring the natural ecosystem. This should be the foundation not only of my own life, but indeed for all humankind.

第2景 太阳鼓舞我自立的梦想

我在心里描绘的是利用太阳、雨水、土地，活用地区特色的生活。那就是尊重生态系，生活上运用动植物的生产力和我们自己产生的各种有机物。这不只是我，也是所有人类生存的根本。

3章「アイトワ 12 節」〜同じ心と出会うまで〜 45

第3節 樹と夢の種をまいた

1958年、大学受験に合格。さまざまな果樹の苗木を20本植えた。そのあとで、土地を4分割することを考えた。果樹、野菜、燃料や建材にする樹木、そして住処に当てよう、と。まず、住処に当てる所から開墾し、サツマイモの畝として活かし始めた。ほどなく養鶏も始めた。

Third View Planted trees and seeds of dreams.

In 1958, I passed my college entrance exams. On our plot of land, I planted 20 fruit trees of assorted varieties, and then determined to divide the land into 4 sections: fruit trees, garden, a wood lot for firewood, and one for the family home. We cleared part of the house lot for a sweet potato bed. Before long we were keeping chickens as well.

第3景 播下树木和梦想的种子

1958年我考上了大学,并种下20棵不同种类的果树幼苗。然后想到要将土地分成四份,分别用于果树、蔬菜、燃料和木材。建造房屋,先开辟住处,作为甘薯的土地活用,然后又开始养鸡。

第4節 大学卒業を目前に、決意を固める

1961年。幹は燃料やシイタケのホタギになり、落ち葉は良き腐葉土になるクヌギの苗木が根づき、順調に育ち始めた。私は、サンショやローリエなどの香木、ナツメやクコなどの薬木に加え、夏は木陰を作り、冬は落葉して日当たりが良くなるカエデやサクラの苗木も植え始めた。もちろん、薬草や山菜も次々と植え、水の自給法も構想した。

 ## Firm resolve at the end of college.

It is 1961. The seedling sawtooth oaks, which we would eventually use for fuel, began to thrive. We added fragrant plants such as prickly ash and bay leaf, medicinal plants such as the jujube tree and false daphne. We planted maples and cherry trees, which would give shade in the summer and shed their leaves in the winter to allow sunlight through. Further, we planted wild edible plants and medicinal plants, and plotted a system for self-sufficient irrigation as well.

第4景 在大学毕业以前下了一大决心

1961年，我种的槲木树苗顺利地落根成长。它的树干可以用于燃料和栽培香菇，落叶能够变成优质的腐土。我又种了花椒树和月桂树等香木以及枣树和露兜树等药树，然后又种了夏天可以成荫，冬天落叶不影响阳光的枫树和樱树。当然也种了不少药草和山菜，还构思了水源的供给方法。

第5節 恵まれた仕事　それでも私は使命を貫く

翌年、23歳。幸いにも大手総合商社に就職できた。父は通勤に便利な所に引っ越すように勧めたが、私はとどまり、住宅金融公庫に融資を申請した。建て増しが容易な小さな家を建てることにしたわけだ。この融資は、私の生涯で、最初で最後の借金となった。

Fifth View: Desirable job. Still faithful to destiny.

The following year, at the age of 23, I was fortunate enough to be hired by a large trading company. My father encouraged me to move to a more convenient location for commuting, but I insisted on staying, and applied to the Housing Loan Corporation for financing to build a house. So, we proceeded to build a small home, which could easily accommodate future additions. This loan was the first and only I have ever taken out.

第5景 条件优越的工作也没有阻止我完成使命

第二年我23岁。幸运地就职于有名的综合商社。虽然父亲建议我搬到离公司近的地方住，以便通勤。可是我没有那样做，而是向住宅金融公库申请贷款。建了一所容易增建的小宅。这次贷款是我一生中第一次，也是最后一次借款。

第6節 使命その1 住宅ローン

1963年、簡素な木造住宅が完成。その後、ほぼすべての収入の余剰分と余暇時間を費やし、「終の棲家」造りにいそしんだ。野菜と燃料が自給できる「自然循環型の空間」創りの始まりだ。後年、この空間を「エコライフガーデン」と呼ぶことになる。

Sixth View: Step One: House loan.

In 1963, we completed the construction of a simple wood-framed house. Subsequently, we invested nearly all of our surplus income and free time into making this home one which would last. This led to the creation of a natural life cycle space where we grow our own vegetables and firewood. In later years, we came to refer to this as our "Eco-life garden."

第6景 第一个使命 贷款盖房

1963年，一所简朴的木材结构的住宅完工了。以后，几乎将所有的收入余额和休假日都毫不吝惜地花在修建这所"终生住居"上。开始创建蔬菜和燃料可以自给自足的"自然循环型的空间"，几年以后把这个空间　称为"生态自然农园"。

第7節 両親もこの地に移り住む

1964年。両親はそれまで住んでいた近くの家を売り払い、その代金で私の家の隣に別棟を造り、越してきた。門扉は私がこしらえた。両親はこの家で、自分の布団で、奇しくも共に満92歳で天に召された。葬儀は家で執り行い、火葬場から持ち帰った遺骨の一部を、この地に散骨した。

Seventh View Parents chose to live here too.

In 1964, my parents sold the house they had been living in nearby, and with the proceeds we built a home for them right adjacent to my house. I had the front entrance gate built. Both of my parents lived in this house until their deaths, which, coincidentally, were both at age 92. We conducted their funerals here and buried a portion of their remains on the property.

 第7景 父母也来此同住

1964年。住在附近的父母将他们的房子卖掉，用卖房子的钱在我家旁边又建了一所房子搬过来住。我为新房亲手做了门窗。父母在这个家，在自己的被子里，奇迹般地活到92岁才去了天堂。他们的葬礼也是在家里举行的。我从火葬场把他们的骨灰拿回来，一部分散在这片土地上。

 第8節 人生を変えたアポロ8号からの光景
　　　　 地球は私たちの唯一の棲家

1969年、アメリカが打ち上げたアポロ8号のおかげで地球を見た。太陽の恵みが地球にとって唯一の収入であることを確信する。1973年、オイルショックを体験。工業社会は早晩破たんするに違いないと覚醒する。ここで、古人の知恵と近代科学の成果を組み合わせ、太陽の恵みの範囲で生きることが、ポスト工業社会（次代）が許す生のありようだと悟り、その現実化に努め始めた。

Eighth View: Life-changing view from Apollo 8: Earth, our one home.

In 1969, I had my first vision of Earth from outer space thanks to Apollo 8. At that moment, it was clear to me that the sun was the sole source of our "revenue." The oil shocks came in 1973. I predicted that "industrial society will eventually go belly-up" and this led me to a major commitment: to combine the wisdom of the ancients and the positive aspects of modern science, in service of a way of life which could be lived within the limits of the sun's energies, and one which could be realized in a post-industrial society.

 第8景 从阿波罗8号宇宙飞船看到的景观
　　　　 ～地球是我们唯一的住处～

1969年，美国发射的阿波罗8号宇宙飞船让我们看到了地球的姿态。使我确信太阳的恩惠是地球唯一的收入。1973年体验了石油冲击（因石油价格的暴涨而引起的经济危机），让我觉醒到工业社会早晚定会毁灭。在此我懂得只有搭配古人的智慧和近代科学的成果，生活在太阳的恩惠范围里才是脱离工业社会（下一代）的应有姿态。为了将它变为现实我正在开始努力。

第9節　同じ心と出会う　人形工房

同じ想いを持つ女性と出会い、結婚した。妻は装飾デザイナーだったが専業主婦になり、庭仕事や両親の世話に勤しんだ。やがて妻は人形創作の世界に踏み出したが、妻にとっては、これこそが人間が生まれながらにして持ち合わせる潜在能力の発露であり、自己実現と思われた。工業社会は「欲望の解放」を促したが、それが環境破壊や資源枯渇などをもたらしたのだろう。来るべき時代は「人間の解放」を、つまり各人固有の良き可能性に目覚める時代に改めるべきだ。

Ninth View: More like-minded people. Doll atelier.

I met and married a woman of like mind. My wife was a fashion designer, but after we married she was fully occupied at home, in the garden, and with the care of my parents. Eventually, she ventured into the world of doll creation. Truly, this was a case of one's unique potential talents revealed and realized. Industrial society promoted "freedom to desire," but to my way of thinking, this has led to nothing but environmental degradation and resource depletion. We ought to transition to "freedom for humanity" in the coming era, in which we realize our own best potential in the renewal of society.

 ## 第9景　相遇知音　人偶制作室

有幸与志同道合的女性相识，结为伴侣。妻子是一位装潢设计师，婚后做了家庭主妇。她辛勤地整理农园，照顾父母，不久还步入创作人偶的艺术世界。显露发挥了她有生的潜在能力，实现了自我。工业社会催促人们"解放欲望"，同时也破坏了自然环境，用尽宝贵的资源。这些使我们醒悟到即将来临的新时代，应该是"解放人类"唤醒每个人特有的可能性的时代。

4章 家屋を「生産の場」から「創造の場」に高める
Elevate Your Home from a Place of "Production" to One of "Creativity"
将住房从"生产的场所"提高到"创意的场所"

工業社会は複製品を大量に生み出し、すべての人を消費者と総称できるようにした。消費者は「消費の喜び」に取り憑かれ、「生産する喜び」を忘れがちになった。その過程で、家屋は「生産する場」から、消費財を買って来て「消費する場」に替えられていたわけだ。

Industrial society gave rise to mass production of replicable goods, and angled to label everyone a consumer. Consumers became obsessed with the "joy of consumption" and tended to overlook the "joy of production." In this process, the home was transformed from a "place of production" to a "place of consumption" of consumer products.

工业社会大量生产复制品，将所有的人都看作消费者。消费者沉醉在"消费的快乐"中，开始忘记"生产的喜悦"。在此过程，房屋从"生产的场所"变成用钱买来消费品"消费的场所"。

幸いなことに、私はこうした社会現象に疑問を抱く多くの人と巡りあえた。妻小夜子は、結婚とは何もかもを独創的に生み出せる新天地を得る機会、と見ていたフシがある。わが家を「生産の場」に留めず、「創造の場」にし始めた。

Fortunately, I have encountered many people who have reservations about this societal phenomenon. My wife, Sayoko, saw marriage as an opportunity to access new territory for creating anything and everything from scratch. She moved beyond making our home a place of production. She made it a place of creativity.

幸而我遇到很多对社会现象带有疑问的朋友。妻子小夜子将婚姻看作能够得到独创一切事物的良机。所以她不仅把家庭当作"生产的场所"，还开始把这里当作"创造的场所"使用。

ホームステイを受け入れるようになり、最初にエリザベス・アームストロングさんと出会えたのも幸いだった。彼女はフロンティアスピリットを両親から授けられ、未来洞察にも優れていた。今ではアメリカの大学で日本語の教授を勤めている。

We were fortunate to have met Elizabeth Armstrong who was our first homestay student many years ago. She inherited the frontier spirit from her parents, and possesses a keen view of the future. She currently teaches Japanese language at a university in the United States.

我们家还欢迎外国人到此寄宿，俗话说有缘千里来相会，伊利莎白・阿姆斯特朗女士是我们接待的第一个外国客人。她继承了父母的开拓精神，对未来具有敏锐的洞察力。目前在美国的大学教授日语。

4章 家屋を「生産の場」から「創造の場」に高める 55

そのようなわけで、この小冊子は、エリザベスさんの協力を得て、日英両言語で作成する運びとなり、ここに至った。その間も、妻は「日本人の基本衣料」を創出したく願うかのような人形を生み出していた。世代を超えて「循環可能な衣服」でもある。

With her cooperation, were we able to produce a trilingual version of this publication. In the meantime, my wife has created dolls which portray "Basic Wear for Japanese" which she hopes will be the future of Japanese clothing. Her vision is of "recyclable wear" which moves beyond generational differences.

这个小册子就是得到伊利莎白女士的协助编译成英文版的。这次翻译成中文版，现在展现给大家阅读。在此期间，妻子已久的愿望"创作日本人的基本服饰"也以人偶的形式问世。这些"可以循环的服饰"超越了世代。

このたび3か国版を作るに当たり、中国訳を劉穎先生に引き受けていただけた。彼女はかつて拙著『次の生き方』を読み、中国訳を思い立ち、訪ねて下さった人だが、その後次第に親交を深めるところとなった人である。

Liu Ying was kind enough to take on the Chinese translation of this publication. Liu Ying read my book *The Next Way of Living* and came up with the notion of a trilingual version. Since then she has become a close friend.

这次将这本书编译成3国语版，担任中文翻译的是刘颖女士。她曾经读《崭新的人生》，然后向我建议翻译成中文，并几次访问爱永远农园，从此逐渐结下深交。

私は、テロのない次代を夢見ている。問題は「文明は、飽食など大量消費をうながすシステムでもある」と考えており、「このシステムの弊害をグローバルに拡大する2次システム（の思想）がグローバリズムであろう」と見ていることだ。つまり、「飽食など大量消費は、その陰で多くの人を餓死などに追いやっているが、それが私の目にはまるで巧妙なテロのように見え始めている」ということだ。

I envision the next era as one free from terrorism. The problem that stands in the way is that Civilization is a system that encourages mass consumption of food, etc. Further, Globalism could be considered a secondary system which expands this detrimental excess worldwide. In other words, mass consumption is driving innumerable people, who remain in its shadow, to starvation. I see this as an insidious form of terrorism.

我的愿望是下一代没有纷争和恐怖。我想问题在于"文明也是促使饱食和大量消费的一个体系"，我认为"将这个体系的弊病扩大到全球的第二体系（的思想）就是全球化的概念。"也就是"受到饱食和大量消费的影响，许多人被逼上死路，甚至饿死。"这些看起来好像一场筹划巧妙的恐怖活动。

「アイトワ 12 節」 ～妻と支え合いながら～
Twelve Views of aightowa: Mutual Support in our Marriage
 爱永远农园12景～与妻子同心协力～

 ### 創作空間を作る

両親に薦められ、エコライフガーデンに、人形工房とカフェを併設した新しい建物を造ることになった。5年がかりで半地下構造の設計プランを練り、次の1年をかけて実現させた。

 ### Construction of creative space.

With the encouragement of my parents, I conceived of a new space in our Eco-life garden comprised of a doll studio and a café. Over the next five years we worked on this plan, and brought it to fruition taking a year to construct this new building with a partially sunken terrace.

建立创作空间

听从父母的建议，在生态自然农园里重新建设了人偶制作室和连在一起的咖啡店。用5年时间制定了半地下构造的建筑计划。然后用以后的1年时间来实现它。

第11節 1986年、アイトワの誕生

新しい建物が完成した。わが家流の生き方で言うと、3世帯分くらいの薪と野菜を供給できる庭もできた。この建物と空間に「アイトワ」との名称を与え、カフェを開いた。これが日本で最初の禁煙ビストロになった。1994年。この屋根に太陽光発電機を設置したが、これは民間家屋が有償設置した日本初の事例になった。

Birth of aightowa, 1986.

In 1986, the new annex was completed. In the spirit of our way of life, we were able to create a garden, which would support about three households with vegetables and wood for fuel. We named our compound **aightowa**. We opened the café and made it the first smoke-free bistro in Japan. Then in 1994, we installed solar panels on the roof of our home, making us the first private residence in Japan to purchase and use these devices.

第11景 1986年 爱永远农园的诞生

新建筑竣工了。以我家的生活方式，这里的农园完全可以供给3代人的烧柴和蔬菜。给这个建筑和空间取名为"爱永远农园"还开设了咖啡店。这里是日本第一个禁止吸烟的咖啡店。1994年，在屋顶设置了太阳光发电机，这也是日本民间房屋第一所安置有偿设施的事例。

エコライフ実践者に引き継ぐまで、薪を割り続ける

この写真は 2005 年。20 年後の 2025 年も私は同じように薪割りをしているだろう。その頃には間違いなく、あらかたの人が「人類はこの 1 つの地球で生きていくしか道はない」と気付いているに違いない。「アイトワ」が、人生を賢明に、真面目に、そして丁寧に送る見本となればと願っている。

 ## Chopping wood until the next generation of Eco-lifers take over.

This photo was taken in 2005. I will probably still be chopping wood in the same way in 2025. I fervently believe that, by that time, there will be many more Eco-lifers who will come to realize that "the only choice for humankind is to continue to live on this singular planet." We hope that **aightowa** will be a beacon for the future of a judicious, earnest and mindful way of life.

 ## 等待实践环保生活的接班人
我会坚持劈柴耕地

这张照片是在2005年拍摄的。20年后的2025年，我一定还在同样劈柴耕地。到了那时肯定大部分的人都会认识到"人类可走的只有这一条在地球生存的道路。"我衷心希望"爱永远农园"成为一个让人生过得聪颖、认真、仔细的模范。

6章 アイトワの時空
The aightowa Cosmos
爱永远农园的时空

1. アイトワのシンボルマーク
aightowa's Logo
"爱永远农园"的标志

赤と緑を基調色に選び、3本の木を配した。赤は「太陽の恵みが地球にとって唯一のインプットである」ことを意識して選び、緑は「愛はいつも新鮮であるべきだ」との願いがエバーグリーンを選ばせた。そして3本の木に、私たちの姓である「森」を形作らせた。

この3本の木に、冬から春の訪れを告げる梅の花、夏に実るドングリ、そして秋の紅葉を描き込むことで「四季の巡り」と「循環」を印象づけようとしている。

また、3本の木に、アイトワとの発音は3つの意味を示すことを暗示させた。それは「愛とは？」「愛と環」そして「愛永遠」の3つである。

Our logo comprises three varieties of trees in complementary red and green hues. We chose the red to symbolize the sun, the only source of power and richness the Earth receives. Green represents the evergreen of love, which should always feel fresh and new. The three trees are arranged to reflect our family name "Mori" (forest) the character for which is composed of three trees (森). These trees suggest the cycle of the four seasons and the cyclical nature of things. The plum blossom is a harbinger of spring, the acorn represents the fruits of summer, and the maple leaf depicts the change of colors in autumn. aightowa, as it is pronounced in Japanese, hints at the meaning of these three symbols: "what is love?," "love and the cycle of life" and "love forever."

标志选择红和绿为基调，搭配3棵树。红色象征"太阳的恩惠对地球来说，是唯一的进口来源。"之所以选择绿色，其中有我的愿望。绿色象征"爱永远保持新鲜不变。"还有3棵树木，合起来就能组成我的姓"森"这个字。在这3棵树上画了从严冬开始报春的梅花、夏季结果的橡子、深秋的红叶，用于描绘"四季的变化"给人留下"循环"的印象。此外，3棵树还暗示了"爱永远农园"的发音"aitowa"里有3个重要的含义。那就是"爱是什么？""爱与和平""爱永远"。

2. エコライフガーデン（アイトワの庭）
Eco-garden (aightowa's garden)
爱永远农园的庭院

アイトワの庭では、200種1000本以上の樹木が育っている。それらはミカンやカキなどの果樹、ゲッケイジュやサンショウなどの香木、カリンやキハダなどの薬木、ウコギやタラなどの食材木、シイタケのホタギになるクヌギ、あるいは観賞木であるモミジやサクラなどであり、それぞれに個別の役割を担わせている。もちろん、無数の草も生えており、さまざまな役割を担っている。
これらの木や草には一体となって美しい景色を構成させるだけでなく、人間の身体だけでなく、魂まで癒す役割を与えている。

There are over a 1000 trees of 200 different varieties growing in **aightowa**'s garden. There are fruit trees such as mikan and persimmon, fragrant plantings such as laurel and prickly ash, medicinal trees such as Chinese quince and cork, edible plants such as ginseng and Japanese angelica. There are oaks where we grow shiitake mushrooms, and trees of beauty like Japanese maples and cherry trees. Each tree has its own unique role to play. Of course, there are innumerable grasses and wild plantings as well, which serve each its own purpose in the garden.
We have composed the landscape of these trees and grasses not only as a unified scene of aesthetic beauty, but also to give solace, to soothe both body and soul.

爱永远农园培育着200种/1000棵以上的树木。有橘子和柿子等果树、月桂和花椒等香树、木梨和黄柏等药树、五加木和楤木等食用树、可以种植香菇的橔木或用来观赏的枫树和樱树等。它们各自具有自己的特点。当然，园内还有无数的花草，它们同样各派用场。
这些树木和花草不但可以组成一幅美丽的风景画面，还可以医治人的身体，放松心灵上的疲劳。

 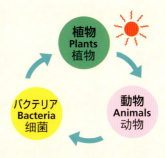

水の循環と潜熱の移動
Water Cycle and Latent Heat Exchange
水的循环和潜热的移动

生態系の概念図
Cycle of life
生态系的概念图

それは、フィトンチッドなど植物の精を振りまきながら空気を浄化し、水の循環（水・液体→水蒸気・気体→水→氷・固体→液体）を促して気温を緩和するなどの他に、これらの木や草に燃料として役立たせた上で、灰を残させるなどの役割である。こうした庭は、人間も自然の一部との認識を抱かせ、家族に医食同源とか身土不二の考え方を大切にさせる。

The landscape cleanses the air through phytoncides emitted by trees, maintains the water cycle, and generally eases the ambient temperature. In addition, we make use of our trees and plants as fuel, which then provide us with ash. This kind of garden green space makes us aware that we are a part of nature, and also makes us mindful of the inseparability of humans and the environment.

具体地说，散布植物杀菌素等植物提炼物有净化空气的作用。还可以促进水的循环（水・液体→水蒸汽・气体→水→冰・固体→液体）缓和气温，除了这些以外，这些树木花草作为燃料也很实用，留下的灰可以做肥料。生活在自然循环的农园，让我们认识到人也是自然的一部分，家里人也很重视医食同源和身土不二的精神。

こうしたさまざまな役割を果たす過程で、これら木や草は、いつしかキリギリスやカマキリ、サワガニやマイマイ、あるいはカエルやヘビなどをこの庭に棲みつかせ、さまざまな小鳥やヤマバト、あるいはイタチやアナグマなどを惹きつけるだけでなく、カラスやサル、あるいはイノシシやシカに襲わせもするようになった。これらの植物と動物は、葉や糞を落としたり、いずれは命がつきたり枯死したりする。それらのいずれもは、やがて土中に棲むミミズやバクテリアなどによって分解され無機物になる。あるいは、燃料となった上で灰を残し、灰も植物の肥料となる。

これら、植物、動物、そして分解者の3者がドラマチックにくりひろげる環は生態系とよばれ、命の環を連綿と繰り返している。私たち人間はこの環の一部に過ぎないが、心身に計り知れない恩恵を与えられる。

The trees and other plants have come to provide a living space for grasshoppers, praying mantis, freshwater crabs, snails, frogs and snakes, as a natural consequence of each of these elements fulfilling its role within the garden. The green space attracts small creatures of all kinds, turtle doves, weasels and badgers. We have been invaded by crows, and even by monkeys and wild boars.

Animals' lives end, plants wither and die, scat and dead leaves fall to the earth; and all of this returns to the soil and is broken down by earthworms and bacteria. Wood becomes fuel from which ashes remain, which is, in turn, useful as fertilizer. This cyclical drama of plants, animals and decomposing agents continuously replays the cycle of life, but also bestows upon us the palpable feeling that human beings are only one small part of this cycle and, indeed, fortunate beyond imagining.

在完成各种作用的过程中，这些树木和花草不知不觉地招来蝈蝈和螳螂、小河蟹和蜗牛、青蛙和蛇等落脚在庭园。农园不仅吸引了各种小鸟和野鸽子，还有黄鼠狼和獾、乌鸦和猴子、而且它们的天敌野猪和鹿会来袭击。这些植物和动物丢下粪便和叶子，什么时候也会丧命枯死。不管怎样，它们在土中会被那里的居民蚯蚓和细菌分解为无机物。或者成为燃料，再变成灰，灰又成为植物的肥料。

这些植物和动物还有分解者成为相互不能缺少的3使者，它们反复上演的循环剧叫做"生态平衡曲"生命之环连绵不断地链接重复着。我们人类只是这个环里的一节，自然赐给我们心身难以衡量的恩惠。

3. エコライフガーデンでのこぼれ話
Eco-garden Fun Facts
爱永远农园庭院的花絮

自生しているフキ、ワラビ、ミョウガ、コゴミ、あるいはセリなど主に栄養源として活かす食草と、ドクダミ、ゲンノショウコ、イカリソウ、あるいはオウレンなど主に薬効分を活かす薬草が、正月7日に食べる七草粥や日常的に風呂で用いる入浴材の材料にもなる。

We cultivate edible plants for our table such as butterbur, bracken fern, wild ginger and ostrich fern. We also use medicinal plants such as fishwort, Thunberg's geranium, horny goat weed, or Japanese goldthread. We use many plants in our traditional foods such as rice porridge with seven spring herbs at New Year's time. We even add herbs to the water in our bath.

自生自长的蜂斗叶、蕨菜、蘘荷、荚果蕨、水芹等都是作为主要营养来源而活用的食用花草。蕺菜、玄草、淫羊藿、黄连等主要作为药效花草来使用，也放在正月7日吃的七草粥里，或者作为入浴材料日常泡澡时使用。

サクラの花が散って一カ月もするとケムシが発生する。「幼虫が固まって葉を食べている間につぶすのが決め手」と妻は無農薬で管理するコツをつぶやきながら、幼虫が群れている葉を見つけて取り、ゴム手袋をはめた指でつぶす。その時期を逃し、少し大きくしてしまうと大変だ。木のあらゆるところに散らばって、すべての葉を食い尽くし始める。

About a month after our cherry trees shed their blossoms, wooly worms begin to appear. "The trick to this is to squash them when the caterpillars are swarming on the leaves," murmured my no-spray wife as she looked for caterpillars and crushed them with the fingertips of her rubber gloves. You have to be vigilant at this stage, since you can get into trouble if the caterpillars get too big. They will spread all over a tree and devastate the leaves.

樱花落后一个月马上生出大量毛虫。以妻子无农药管理的经验"幼虫聚在一起吃叶子的时候是消灭它们的好时机"，她一边谈经验，一边戴上胶皮手套寻找带有

很多幼虫的叶子，把它们用手套指尖捏死。如果错过这个时期的话，虫子长大就麻烦了！那样会扩散到树的每个地方，把所有叶子吃得精光。

愛犬は、鎖でつながれているときは器に入れて与えた水道水を飲むが、庭に放たれたり、散歩をさせたりしている時は、庭の随所にある水槽や水鉢に溜まった自然水を飲む。そこで、庭にやってくる野鳥やケモノのために、その水飲み場にし易い水槽なども用意している。

Our dog drinks water from the water dish we provide when he is tied up outside, but he drinks rain water caught in various containers when he is let loose in the garden or when we go for a walk. We also have water containers placed about from which birds and wildlife can drink as well.

爱犬用链子拴着的时候，喝我们为它准备的倒在盆里的自来水。放养在农园里或带它去散步的时候，它会自己寻找农园里随处放着的水槽或水盆里的积水喝。我们为光临农园的野鸟和野兽准备了一些水槽，让它们容易找到饮水的地方。

色づいたカリンの実は良い香りがする。喉が弱い私は、この実でカリン酒を作り、ウォッカと半々に割って常備薬にする。それをミニボトルに詰めて持ち歩き、講義などで喉が痛むとひと舐めする。カリン酒を造るときにカリンを切り裂くと、農薬を使っていないから虫がよく出てくる。その虫に襲われた実の方がより体に効くカリン酒を造らせるものと信じている。

The fruit of the colorful Chinese quince has a lovely fragrance. Prone to sore throats, I regularly take our homemade quince wine in combination with vodka for medicinal purposes. I carry a flask of this mixture, and when my throat is sore from speaking engagements I take one small dose. When we cut open the quinces for wine-making, we usually discover bugs inside as we use no pesticides. I think that the fruit invaded by pests allows me to make quince wine which is more medicinally effective.

成熟的木梨不但颜色好看，还带有很好的果香。嗓子爱疼的我用它做成木梨酒，作为常备药加上一半伏特加酒服用。有时把它倒入小瓶拿出去，讲课伤了喉咙感到疼痛的时候就喝一小口。因为不用农药，做木梨酒，切开果实的时候常会掉出虫子。我深信被虫子喜爱的木梨一定对人的身体也很好，所以做果实酒不能缺少虫子的存在。

父の助言で植えた1本のタケから小さな竹藪を造った。まず竹をはびこらせたくないところに出たタケノコは採って食材にする。タケの皮は中華ちまきやサバ寿司などを造るときに欠かせない。タケは蔓性野菜の支柱や、花壇の縁取りにも生かす。落葉は、夏野菜がマルチングを求める頃から始まり、その用が済めば鋤き込み、肥料にする。使用済みのタケは風呂の焚きつけにし、残った灰は肥料にする。

My father encouraged me to grow a small bamboo grove, which I did starting with just one tree. We harvest new bamboo shoots for our table from areas in which we do not want the bamboo to spread. The outer leaves of the bamboo shoots are essential when making Chinese-style rice packages and pressed mackerel sushi. We use bamboo as stakes for vine vegetables and as greenery for flowerbeds. Leaves begin to fall just when the summer vegetables require mulching, and when the leaves have served that purpose we compost them to make fertilizer. Leftover bamboo branches we use as kindling for heating the wood-fired bath, and then those ashes too become fertilizer.

父亲建议我种植的一棵竹子，现在竟长成一片小竹林。我们摘采竹笋的时候，选择不希望竹子长得太茂盛的地方摘，然后拿回去做菜。竹子皮是包粽子或青花鱼寿司时不可缺少的材料。此外，竹子还能支撑藤蔓蔬菜、为花坛周围搭起栅栏。落叶从覆盖栽培夏季蔬菜的时期就开始发挥作用，过后耕耘又可作为肥料使用。用过的竹子还可加热浴盆，剩下的灰又能变成肥料。

「カブトムシの引っ越しのお手伝いをしているみたい」とつぶやきながら、妻はカブトムシの幼虫を傷つけやすいスコップやフォークを使わず、軍手をはめた手で腐葉土をかき出し、一輪車に積み込む。野鳥やケモノがカブトムシの幼虫を狙って腐葉土小屋をよく襲うが、私たちはある時はカブトムシの幼虫の、またある時はトリやケモノの味方をしており、それはどうしてかと、ときどき考えこまされる。

"It is as if I'm helping the beetles with a home move," mumbled my wife as she gathered up the rotting leaves and put them in the wheelbarrow with her gloved hands rather than using a rake or shovel which could injury the beetle larvae. Birds and wild animals often attack the leaf bin to get these larvae. Sometimes we side with the beetles and sometimes with the birds and animals, and often are at a loss as to why we feel this way.

妻子边说："你看我好像在帮助独角仙搬家吧！"边戴上线手套，用手来挖腐土放到单轮车里。她不轻易用叉子和铁锹是为了不伤害独角仙的幼虫。野鸟和野兽经常为了获取独角仙的幼虫而前来袭击装腐土的小屋，我们有时保护独角仙，有时也为野鸟和野兽着想。为什么这样做？连我们自己也很难回答。

薪風呂や薪ストーブは、枯れた杉の葉と細く割った枯れた竹があればマッチ1本ですぐに点火し、簡単に太い薪を燃え上がらせる。だが、冬に薪風呂を焚き上げるには2時間もかかる。だから私は、妻の展示会が近づいたりすると妻に代わって焚き、感謝される。妻に代わって焚くようになり、私は長風呂になったが、妻は何かを言いたげだ。

We can light our wood-fired bath heater and our wood stove with one match when we use dried cedar leaves or dried bamboo split for tinder, which then makes it easier to burn larger logs. That said, it takes up to two hours to get the bath heated to temperature during the winter. When one of my wife's doll exhibitions is imminent, I take over the job of getting the fire started and burning well. She appreciates this. Yet, when I take over, the bath takes longer. My wife seems to have an opinion about this, but keeps her peace.

用柴火烧洗澡水和火炉时，只要有干枯的杉树叶子和砍得细细的枯竹，然后马上用火柴点火的话，再粗的柴也容易烧起来。可是，冬季要想烧洗澡水的话，竟然需要2个小时。所以妻子的展览会即将到来的时候，我将代替她的工作烧水，妻子对此十分感谢。代替妻子烧水以后，我开始长时间泡澡。看到这些妻子好像要对我说些什么。

太陽の恵みを最も簡単に活かす工夫としてさまざまなタイプの天窓（トップライト）を9カ所に配した。その1つは、植物の力を組み合わせることで、冬は温室のような暖かさが、夏は木陰のような涼しさがえられるようにした。

We have installed skylights in nine locations in our buildings, which is one of the easiest ways to harness the power of the sun. This combines with the power of our trees to give us the warmth of a greenhouse in the winter and cool shade in the summer.

我在家里的9个地方下工夫安装了容易活用阳光的各种样式的天窗。其中一个利用了植物的特长，结果冬天像温室一样暖和，夏季可以享受树荫般的凉爽。

生ゴミは、収穫を終えたキュウリやエンドウマメの蔓など畑から出る残り物を井桁のように積み上げ、その中央に放り込み、共に自然分解させて堆肥にする。種を結んだ野草などは燃やして灰にする。燃えにくい根や球根など、灰にも堆肥にもしにくいものを放り込む穴もある。この穴には、割れた植木鉢なども砕いて放り込み、いずれは樹木の根が好む肥料分に富んだ、しかも水はけのよい土になる。ガラス、紙、プラスチック、あるいは金属など他のゴミは資源ゴミとしてそれらの受け入れ施設に届ける。

We toss our wet compost into a hole in the middle of the piles of vines removed from the garden. Natural decomposition gives us compost. We burn weeds that still carry their seeds to make more ash. We also have a hole into which we throw those roots and bulbs which are hard to burn and hard to make into compost. We crush broken planters and toss them in this hole as well. Both of these allow the rich water to enhance the soil which feeds tree roots. We recycle glass, paper, plastic and metals at the appropriate recycling facility.

关于垃圾的处理，我们将收获的黄瓜和豌豆的蔓等从田里取出堆成"井"字，垃圾就扔进中间，让它们一起自然分解堆肥。结了种子的野草等要烧成灰，不好烧的根部和球根等不容易成灰和堆肥，就把这些东西投入坑里处理。专用坑里也扔打碎的花盆，把它们砸碎后放进去，以后可以变成树根喜爱的肥料和容易排水的泥土。玻璃、废纸、塑料、还有金属等属于其他垃圾，这些作为资源垃圾运到可以接收的专门设施。

排水は、屎尿、生活雑排水、そして雨水の３つに分別しており、洗剤など化学物質を含んだ排水以外は庭で活かす。複数あるトイレはいずれも水洗式だが、家族用は、その先に設置した大きな地下タンクに流れ込み、自然発酵し、肥料として活かされる。喫茶店など来客用の複数のトイレは、地下タンクには流れ込まず、それらの汚水は下水道に捨て去る。だから外食などが続き、添加物や抗生物質などを多量にとりこんだと家族が思ったときは、家族用のトイレは使用しない。（ちなみに、雨水は、カフェテラスと屋根の多くの部分に降り注いだ分は下水道に捨て去る。畑、庭、あるいは屋上緑化部分はもとより、一部の屋根に降り注いだ分は、その多くは庭で活かす。風呂の残り湯も渇水期には庭の散水に活かす）

Our wastewater is separated into three categories, sewage, gray water and rainwater. We use all of these on our garden, except water which contains agents such as detergent. The toilets in our home flow into a large underground tank where the wastewater ferments, and we then use it as fertilizer. The sewage from toilets to which customers have access in the café does not flow into the same underground tank, but rather is siphoned off to the sewer system. Therefore, when any member of our family has consumed large amounts of additives or antibiotics from eating out for a period of time, we do not use the household toilets. (As a footnote, most of the rain water which flows off the roof of the café is directed to the sewer system. Rainwater which is collected in the garden, green space and some sections of our roofs is used in our garden. We also use our bath water on the garden during dry spells.)

农园的排水分成屎尿、生活排水、雨水这3种，除了含有洗涤剂等化学成分的排水以外都活用于农园。园内的几个厕所虽然都是抽水式，家用厕所流入先端设置的大型地下槽里自然发酵，然后作为肥料使用。咖啡店等来客用的几个厕所不流入地下槽，这些污水顺着下水道排去。如果我们接连在外边吃饭，觉得体内吸收了很多添加剂或抗生素等的时候，就不用自家厕所。（顺便提一下，浇在咖啡店屋顶和屋檐的雨水也顺着下水道排去。浇在田地、庭园、还有屋顶绿化部分和一部分屋檐的雨水，大部分都活用于农园。洗澡剩下的温水也留在干季洒在农园。）

7章 未来の夢

1. アイトワを創出した想い

　最大多数の最大幸福という言葉がある。私はいつしか、この言葉の最大多数に未来世代を含めて考えるようになり、次第に私は生き方を変えた。これが太陽の恵みの範囲で豊かに生きる夢を追い求めさせるようになった。化石資源とは、植物が太陽の恵みを炭素化合物にしてため込んだ代物であり、地球にとってはいわば定期預金のようなものだ、と気付いたからだ。その活かし方は、未来世代の得心が不可欠ではないか。

バイオロジカルエコロジーの概念

　工業社会は、化石資源などを好き放題に使い、世界中の人々がまねたら地球をたちまちにして破壊しかねない生き方を広めて来た。また、非現実の世界を体験する装置とも言うべきディズニーランドも誕生させた。だが、次の社会は、世界中の人々がまねたら、人々の生活をより豊かにするだけでなく、同時に自然を復元させる現実的なテーマパークを創出させざるをえなくなるに違いない。そう私は信じるようになり、小さくともその1つのモデルを創出したくなり、家族を巻き込んで取り組んできた。

　それは、「古人の生きる知恵」と「近代科学が生み出す成果物」を巧みに活かすことで現実化させることにした。なぜなら、あらかたの人に「これなら」とすぐにでも受け入れられ、馴染んでもらえないといけない、と考えたからだ。かくして、私たち家族は既製品の消費を控え、創造的に生きるリビングシステムを創出した。そしてこの自然循環型生活空間に、「アイトワ」という総称を与え、庭には「エコライフガーデン」との愛称を与えた。

　同時に、望ましき次の社会のコンセプトを十分に語れるようになったと思ったので、喫茶室を喫茶店に改装し、1986年4月5日から一般開放した。「アイトワ」の自然循環型生活を「バイオロジカルエコロジー」と呼ぶことにして、この普及を夢見て提唱し始めた。

2. 未来の夢

　工業社会はいずれ破綻する、と私は睨み、次の社会を夢見て来た。だから私生活では「バイオロジカルエコロジー」を追求したわけだが、それでは片手落ちだと気付かされるようになった。なぜなら、次の生き方が必要とする品物やサービスなどが市場には欠けており、企業にも次の社会を夢見てもらう必要がある、と思うに至ったからだ。

インダストリアルエコロジーの概念

　そこで1995年にアメリカ取材もしており、1つのヒントを得ている。それは「インダストリアルエコロジー」という概念であった。A社の廃棄物をB社が原料にする。B社の廃棄物をC社が原料にする。こうしてZ社に至り、Z社からA社につながるがごとくに、社会全体として自己完結する企業社会である。つまり、地下資源に頼らず、地上にある資源だけで社会がまかなえるようにする企業社会である。

　この時点で、私の瞼に次代のあるべき姿がありありと浮かぶようになった。それは「バイオロジカルエコロジー」と「インダストリアルエコロジー」が手をつなぎ、日々の太陽の恵みの下で、地球を復元させながら、人類をより人間らしい生き方に誘う時代の姿である。それを「第4時代」と呼ぶことにした。

　なぜなら、人類史は原始時代から始まり、次の農業文明時代を経て第3の時代である工業文明時代に至ったが、これらに次ぐ時代を創出した場合の姿であるからだ。

　第3時代は、人類が「他の動物と共有する部分」の開発を過度に押し進めてきた。それは行き過ぎた「欲望の解放」であり、工業社会が生み出す複製品の大量消費を促した。

第4時代の概念図

　それに対して、第4時代は「人類固有の部分」の開発を希求する時代である。各人が持って生まれた固有の潜在能力を尊び、その発露を願い「人間の解放」を希求する時代である。それは人類のみに許されている創造能力や未来洞察能力などの活性化に目覚め、発露し合い、相互の好意と敬意の社会と言い直せる。自己実現を希求しあう社会である。
　近年では、かつて日本が体験した江戸時代の研究が進んでいる。その内の300年近くは、人口3000万人程度で静止した閉鎖（鎖国）社会であった。そこで繰り広げられていた社会の姿が次第に明らかになってきたが、私は第4時代の概念を考える上で注視している。少なくともその文化は、地球という閉鎖空間で、生きとし生けるものが肩を寄せ合っておだやかに生きる知恵を多く含んでおり、「古人の生きる知恵」の最も有力なモデルである。
　中国は「遊」という文字も生み出した。それは「完全な自由」と「創造能力」を兼ね備えた活動のひと時を意味しており、「人間の解放」のひと時と見てよいのではないか。近年、江戸時代の人々が、その多くの時間を、この「遊」の概念に基づくオリジナリティ豊かな生き方に費やしていたことが明らかになりつつある。

7章　未来の夢　75

7章 The Future Dream

1. Concepts Which Gave Rise to aightowa

There is a saying: the greatest happiness for the greatest number. At some point, I began to give this saying a great deal of thought, considering future generations among "the greatest number." Gradually, I have changed my way of life. This spurred me on to pursue the dream of living a rich life within the limits of what the sun graciously provides us.

Petroleum resources are nothing more than carbon compounds from plants made from solar energy; in short, from the Earth's perspective, a certificate of deposit. To my way of thinking, how we use these resources depends on the stance and behavior of future generations.

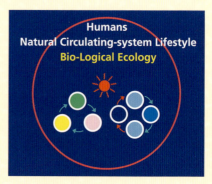

Bio-Logical Ecology

Industrial society has propagated a way of living which encourages unlimited use of petroleum resources, but this will destroy the world swiftly if everyone across the globe imitates it. It gave birth to such phenomena as Disneyland, which can be described as a mechanism for experiencing the world of unreality. The next society will not only make our lives more rich and abundant if shared across the world, but surely will also simultaneously give rise to "reality" theme parks that will restore and reconstitute nature in its most natural form. I have come to believe and pursue this, enlisting the efforts of my family as well.

I have chosen to make this happen by carefully synthesizing "the wisdom of the ancients" with the "fruits of modern science." I hope that anyone and everyone can embrace the concept of this synthesis. We labeled our living space, as a system, **aightowa**, and called our growing space the Eco-life garden. We felt we were ready and able to share our thoughts on what I refer to as the "next society," so we remodeled our tearoom into a café and opened it to the public on April 5, 1986. We called this natural circulating-system lifestyle "Bio-Logical Ecology" and began to advocate for this kind of life.

2. The Future Dream

I have despaired of industrial society, assuming that it will eventually fail, and have dreamed of the next society ever since. Thus, I have pursued the Bio-Logical Ecology style of personal life, and yet still I have been forced to realize that this is an untenable stance. This is because I realized that there are insufficient goods and services in the marketplace necessary to make this next way of life possible, and because it is necessary for industry to embrace this dream of the future as well.

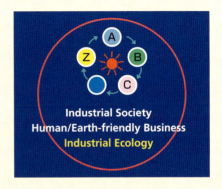

Industrial Ecology

To this end, in 1995, I traveled to the United States to collect information on this topic, and was able to obtain one important hint in particular. That was the notion of "Industrial Ecology." Company A's waste products become the raw materials for Company B. Company B's waste products are used as Company C's raw materials. This goes along all the way through to Company Z which leads back to Company A, and thus it creates an industrial society as a whole entity which is self-completing; in other words, an industrial society which does not rely on subterranean resources, but rather provides for itself using only that which is garnered from the Earth's surface.

Soon the notion of how the next industrial society should be became abundantly clear to me. It is a society in which Bio-Logical Ecology and Industrial Ecology join hands to restore the Earth, with the benevolence of the sun; and invites the human race to live more as human beings. This is what I call "the 4th epoch."

Human history began with primitive times, moved on to the agricultural age and then the industrial age, the 3rd epoch. The 4th epoch expresses the character of the age that created it. In the 3rd epoch, humanity indulged in the excessive development of "what we share communally with other animals." It was an exaggerated expression of "unleashed desire," and encouraged mass consumption of industrial replicable products.

7 The Future Dream 77

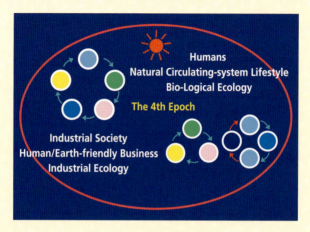

The 4th Epoch

In contrast, the 4th epoch is an age in which there is longing for and pursuit of development of "that which is inherently human." It is an age in which we honor the innate potential capability of each person, and strive for "human liberation" as an expression of that desire. This will give rise to a society, which will realize and manifest revitalization of creative powers and powers of discernment granted only to human beings, one which we can aptly call a society based on mutual amity and regard. It will be a society in which we all can strive for self-realization.

In recent years, advances have been made in research initiated during Japan's Edo period (1603~1868). For nearly 300 years, Japan was a closed country with a population stable at about 30,000,000. That society's character gradually manifested itself as it developed, but I focus close attention on it particularly in light of the concept of the 4th epoch. At very least, that civilization embodied the wisdom of those who could and would live together peacefully shoulder to shoulder. It was a powerful model of "the wisdom of the ancients."

China created the character 遊 (yū: play). This character means a moment in time when there is synthesis of "complete freedom" and "creative ability." Couldn't we consider "human liberation" precisely that kind of moment? Nowadays it has become increasingly clear how much time people of the Edo period devoted to a rich and unique way of life based on the concept of 遊 (yū).

7 The Future Dream

7章 未来的梦想

1. 我为什么创建"爱永远农园"

生物生态学的概念

有这样一句话:"最大多数的最大幸福"(杰里米·边沁的英国功利主义理论。幸福属于个人的快乐,社会是个人的总体,最大多数人的最大快乐才是人类应该追求的目标。)我认为这句话里的"最大多数"包括未来的世代,这样我的生活有了变化。也让我有了一个梦想,就是在太阳的恩惠范围里幸福地生活。因为我觉察到化石资源是植物将太阳的恩惠化为碳化合物的取代物品,对地球来说就像定期存款一样。怎样活用它,应该取得未来世代的同意。

工业社会随心所欲地使用化石资源,并将此生活不断扩大,全世界的人如果都模仿的话,地球很快就会灭亡。此外发明了很多体验非现实世界的装置,比如说迪斯尼乐园的诞生等。但是,如果全世界的人都模仿以下我提议的社会,人们的生活会更富有,同时不但可以恢复自然,还可以创建现实的主题游乐园。我这样深信,于是想创建一个即使小也可以成为模范的例子,就这样全家投入了这项工程。

我们将"古人的生活智慧"和"近代科学发明的成果"巧妙地活用于现实。因为想到只有这样做,大部分的人才可能马上接受,让大家习惯它,认为 "啊,要是这样我也能做到!"从那以后,我们家在消费上尽量少用现成的东西,以创建自力更生的生活系统。然后将这个自然循环型的生活空间称为"爱永远农园",给农园起了一个爱称:"环保生活庭园"。

同时感到应该把农园作为理想社会的系统好好做宣传。下一步将咖啡屋改修成咖啡店,于1986年4月5日一般开放。还把"爱永远农园"的自然循环型的生活叫做"生物生态学"并且以普及为目标开始提唱这里的生活。

2. 未来的梦想

工业社会早晚要瘫痪，我带着这个想法幻想着新的社会。所以在自己的生活里追求"生物生态学"的理念，但是又感到只这些会有点偏向。因为新的人生所需要的物品和服务等都是市场不具备的，企业同样有必要面对新的社会，努力去实现它。

1995年我去美国采访时得到1个提示："工业生态学"的概念。例如，B公司把A公司的废弃物当原料。C公司把B公司的废弃物当原料。这样一直

工业生态学的概念

到Z公司，就像从Z公司链接A公司一样，作为整体社会来实现自己的企业。也就是说，企业要做到不依赖地下资源，只利用地上资源就能实现新的社会。

在这个阶段，我的眼里浮现出下一代应有的姿态，一个召唤时代的姿态。那就是"生物生态学"和"工业生态学"携手在太阳的恩惠下，一边使地球康复，一边让人类生活得更富有人性和个性。我把它叫做"第4时代"。

因为，人类的历史从原始时代开始，然后经历了农业文明时代，后来到达第3时代，就是现在的工业文明时代。"第4时代"是继承前几代应有的姿态。

第3时代，人类推进"与其他动物共有部分"的过度开发。那些都是越轨的"欲望解放"，并促进了工业社会生产复制品进行大量消费。

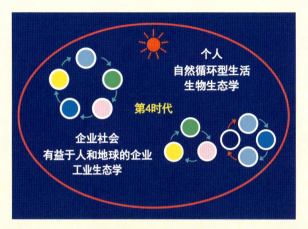

第4时代的概念图

  与第3时代相比较，第4时代是开发希求"人类固有部分"的时代，尊重个人天生固有的潜在能力，希望发掘它，希求"人类解放"的时代。那是只有人类才具备的创造力和对未来的洞察力。换句话说，要激活和唤醒这些，相互显露，相互抱有敬意和好感的社会，是希求实现自我的社会。

  近年，对过去日本经历的江户时代的研究十分活跃。其中将近300年人口静止在3000万人左右，这就是锁国（江户政府禁止基督教进入日本，也不允许日本人出境和入境。并且严格管理统治和限制贸易的对外政策）的社会。通过研究渐渐看清了这个时代展开的社会画卷，我在思考第4时时代的概念上对此十分注目。至少这个时期的文化对地球这个封闭的空间，提供了很多作为生物大家应该怎样并肩共存的智慧，是"古人生存智慧"中最有力的模范。

  中国创造了"遊"这个文字。它的意思是兼备"完全自由"和"创造能力"的活动时间，也可以看作"人类解放"的时间。近年的研究证实了江户时代的人们把很多时间以这个"遊"的概念为基础，花在创建富有个性的生活上。

7章 未来的梦想

Memories of aightowa

In the fall of 1977, I was paired with Takayuki and Sayoko Mori as their home stay student. This fortuitous event changed the trajectory of my life. The Moris took me into their home for a year when I was a junior in college, and treated me as if I were their own daughter. The director of the aboard program I participated in told me that he had given me the best home stay family, and he was right. They opened their home and hearts to a complete stranger, shared their passions and curiosities, and taught me the value of the intangible.

In the United States, I had been raised doing much of the work that the Moris enjoyed and valued on their property such as gardening and wooding. I remember the first time Mr. Mori took me out to the wood pile and offered me a chance to split wood with him. I had been chopping wood from childhood and I think he was rather surprised by this 19-year girl who ripped through knotty logs. We bonded strongly during this and other daily activities of the self-sufficient life they had chosen. We planted, cultivated and reaped the year-round bounty of the garden. We talked of weighty things, to the extent that my then rudimentary Japanese of that time would allow. They included me in all things great and small from washing dishes together to felling a mighty tree in their compound.

Over the course of nearly 40 years, I have had the privilege of maintaining my friendship with the Moris. Mr. Mori gave me my first job out of college. They acted as my home base whenever I traveled to Japan or lived in other parts of the country. Mr. Mori hired me as his guide and interpreter to tour the United States, when he was working on a book about the "new" concepts of business for social responsibility, conservation and the eco-life. When they opened the café **aightowa**, we discussed the spelling of the name, and then they asked my mother to do the original calligraphy. In recent years, I have brought a group of college students to his home to learn about the exemplary and unusual life he and his wife lead here; a life of self-sufficiency, spiritual satisfaction, and kindness to the earth.

It has been my great, good fortune to know the Moris. I look forward to many more years of this special relationship with my second set of parents.

Elizabeth Armstrong. October 2018

アイトワでの思い出

1977 年の秋に、留学生として孝之さんと小夜子さんのお宅でお世話になりました。この
ホームスティの経験が私の人生の方向を完全にかえてしまいました。

大学三年の時でしたが、森夫妻は、私を自分の娘かのように受け入れてくださいました。
留学プログラムの所長に、「一番いいホームスティ先と組んであげたよ」と言われましたが、
まさにその通りでした。見も知らぬアメリカの娘を暖かく迎え入れ、情熱や好奇心をとも
に分かち合い、「こころ」の価値を教えてくださいました。

アメリカで生まれ育った私は、孝之さんと小夜子さんが生活の柱としてやっている庭作
りや薪割りを子供のころからやっていましたので、はじめから気が合ったというか、趣味
が合いました。孝之さんが初めて薪割りをやってみないかと勧めて下さった時をよく覚え
ています。そこで私は、斧を裏がえして割りにくい薪を打つ技を用いてやったところ、孝
之さんが「うん」と頷いてくださったことをよく覚えています。森夫婦ならではの自給自
足の生活をともに送りながら、徐々に強い絆を築いて行きました。年から年中、種を植え、
土を培い、また収穫するサイクルで一緒に畑仕事をさせていただいたりしました。草ぬき
や果樹の世話を一緒にしながら、当時の私の初歩的な日本語が許す限り、重要な課題を語
り合いました。お皿洗いから大木を倒して処理する作業にいたるまで身内のように参加さ
せていただきました。

孝之さんと小夜子さんとのお付き合いはもはや 40 年近くなっています。孝之さんは大
学を卒業したての私を日本に招請し、勤めている会社の部下として雇ってくださいました。
その後、アメリカから往来しているころ、時々「里帰りもして、短期間の居候（？）もさ
せていただきました。そして孝之さんが 1990 年代のアメリカの環境保護運動、社会的責
任を持つ企業、持続可能な生き方や企業のあり方といったテーマで本を書かれることに
なった時には、市場調査および通訳を頼まれました。ご一緒したその出張も意味深い思い
出になっています。

また、アイトワのカフェを開店する前に、「アイトワ」という横文字をどういったスペ
ルにすべきかと相談されました。一味違ったスペルが決まってから、グラフィック・デザ
イナーをやっていた私の母が看板の文字を得意のカリグラフィーで原本を書かせていただ
きました。ほんのわずかですが、こういったところで、森夫妻の生活や活躍に参加してき
ました。最近は、私の大学の教え子を対象に行った研修旅行を通じて、自給自足、心の満
足、地球に優しい生活、すなわち森夫婦がお手本として見せてくださる生活様式を紹介し
ました。

孝之さんと小夜子さんと知り合いになり、長い年月にわたってお付き合いさせていただ
いたことを心から感謝しています。日本の「両親」との特別な関係をこれからずっと続け
て行きたいと思っています。

2018 年 10 月　エリザベス・アームストロング

爱永远农园的回忆

1977年秋天，我作为留学生来到孝之先生和小夜子女士的家里寄宿。这个寄宿经历完全改变了我的人生方向。

那是在我上大学三年的时候，森夫妇把我当作自己的女儿来看。记得留学计划所长对我说："我们给你安排了一个最好的寄宿家庭。"正像他所说的一样，夫妇俩人热情地迎接我这个陌生的美国女孩，与我一起分享激情和好奇心，教给我"真心善意"的价值。

虽然我在美国出生长大，但从小就在家习惯于砍柴和造园等体力劳动。这些也是孝之先生和小夜子女士生活里必不可少的内容。所以开始我们相处得就很投机，兴趣爱好也很相似。我清楚地记得，孝之先生最初让我"你试试砍柴怎么样？"我二话没说就拿起斧子瞄准方向把难劈的木头劈成柴，孝之先生点头称赞"嗯，不错！"

我和森夫妇一起度过农园独特的自给自足的生活，不知不觉地和他们建立了深厚的感情。整整一年里播种、培土、收获，这个过程都在地里一起干活。有时还一边拔草，护理果树，一边使用当时我能说的初级日语和他们谈论重要的课题。不管是洗盘子，还是砍倒大树，无论什么体力活都像一家人似的参加。

现在和孝之先生和小夜子女士的交往已经有40年了。孝之先生还把刚刚大学毕业的我邀请回日本，雇用我做他公司的部下。那以后，每当我往来于日美之间，时时会像"回娘家，小住几日"的形式再次与他们重逢。

孝之先生写了几本关于1990年代美国的环境保护运动、企业的社会责任、可以持续的生活方式和理想企业等主题的书籍。那时他让我做他的翻译，一起出差搞市场调查也给我留下了深刻的印象。此外，爱永远咖啡厅开店以前，他和我商量应该把"爱永远"横写为什么字母。决定与众不同的字母以后，做过装潢设计工作的母亲把咖啡店的招牌写成她很擅长的美术字。这些虽然是几件小事，能够参加和参与森夫妇的生活和工作，我感到十分荣幸。

最近通过以我大学学生为对象的研修旅行，介绍了自给自足、心灵上的满足、保护地球的生活，这些也就是以森夫妇为模范的生活形式。有缘与孝之先生和小夜子女士相识，我从心里感谢能够和他们如此长期的交往。并希望和日本"双亲"的亲密关系从此也能长久持续。

2018年10月　伊利莎白·阿姆斯特朗

春を待つアイトワ
aightowa anticipating spring
盼望春天的爱永远农园

「エピローグ」 〜清豊を夢見て〜

　中国は「第 18 次全人代」で「五位一体」を打ち出し、その 1 つが「エコ文明」であったことを知り、感動しました。さらに、その中国語表記が「生態文明」だと劉穎先生に教わり、しかもその仕組みが「経済が根本、政治が保証、文化が霊魂、社会が条件、そして生態文明が基礎」と定義されていると知らされ、これは全人類が心がけて取り組まなくてはならないスローガンだと思い、とても感銘しました。と同時に、少し悔しい思いもしています。それはどうしてか。

　1986 年に私は、恵まれた給与所得生活と決別し、著作に手を付けました。処女作『ビブギオールカラー　ポスト消費社会の旗手たち』が日の目を見たのはバブルという言葉が流布する前でした。主旨は、工業時代に次ぐ時代（「第 4 時代」と呼ぶにとどめた）を創出し、移行しようとの提唱であり、勤労者には次代の旗手・ビブギオール（紫の V から始まり赤の R で終わる虹の頭文字）カラーになろうとの呼びかけでした。だが、バブルに酔い始めた人たちには見向きもされませんでした。

　やがて工業社会は、危惧した通りに単色のホワイトカラーやブルーカラーのリストラ（追放）を始めました。他方、中国を始めとする多くの国が工業文明への移行を本格化していました。その時に私は、19 世紀半ばのイギリスで、ウイリアム・モリスが残した言葉を思い出します。工業社会は、農業社会の奴隷や中世の農奴よりも惨めな賃金労働者を生み出すであろうとの予言です。

　その後、ある女子短期大学から招聘され、その使命は定員割れが必定だった学校の再興でした。もちろん私は、持論の「3 匹目のネコになれ」との標語も叫んでおり、10 年後に去りましたが、その時は全学科の入学者数が定員をオーバーしていました。在学生が卒業した高校に、あるいは後輩に「この学校は良い」と推奨していたのです。

〜 3 匹目のネコになれ（2006 年 3 月 3 日）〜

　世の中では新入学生を迎え入れる準備で忙しい季節になりました。そのせいか、私はかつて学生にしばしば「キミたちは何匹目のネコになろうとしているんだ」と喝を入れたことを思い出しました。これだけ言えば通じる話を学生に「環境論」などの講義の時間などで講じてあったからです。

　「いつも魚をくれる人を、優しい人だと思うようでは並のネコだ。その人は、本当は怖い人だ。魚の捕り方を忘れかねないネコにする恐れがある。ならば魚の捕り方を教

える人を優しい人と見てよいのか」と問いかけました。続きはこうです。

「違う。この人も怖い人だ。それが資源枯渇問題などを生じさせたことに気付くべきだ。君たちには、魚の生態を教える人を本当に優しい人だと見抜く三匹目のネコになってほしい。魚とどのように付き合えば、魚を永続的に増やしながら自分も幸せになれるのか、そのコツを住み着いた環境で自分なりに会得する賢いネコになってほしい」（以下省略）　　　　（産経新聞コラム「自活のススメ」20060303、原題「3匹目のネコ」）

　一匹目のネコは、農業社会が生み出したネコです。二匹目のネコは、工業社会が限りなく追い求めたネコではありませんか。学生には「工業時代」に次ぐ「第4時代」の到来に備え、生態系に配慮できる「三匹目のネコになれ」と呼びかけたわけです。

　それだけに、中国の五位一体を人類共通の目標と見て感動し、同時に私はなぜ「第4時代」を「生態時代」と呼んでおかなかったのか、と残念に思ったのです。「生態時代」は「生態文明」が切り拓くわけですが、その決め手は「文化」を「霊魂」と位置付けることだと確信していたからです。人類は、工業文明から「生態文明」に移行する上で克服しなければならない課題を抱えており、そこで不可欠となるのが霊魂です。この想いは拙著『次の生き方』では「文明の怖さと文化の大切さ」との見出しをつけて触れています。

　こうした意識は、習近平国家主席が2017年の共産党大会で延べた「中国の特色ある社会主義の政治制度は偉大なる創造である。我々は人類の政治文明の進歩に貢献する自信と能力が備わっている」との認識に触れ、共鳴しました。この是非はともかく、今や私たちはさまざまな主義、宗派、あるいは肌の色などを乗りこえ、手を携えて人類共通の敵に立ち向かわなければならない時なのです。

　その敵は、幾万年か前にアフリカを旅立ち、今や地球のあらゆるところで分け住まうようになった現生人類の、とりわけ工業文明圏に住まう私たちの心に巣くっているのです。それはアダム・スミスがいう「自愛心に基づく見えざる手」への偏重でしょう。私たちはもう片方の手を有していたことを見直し、それを有効かつ存分に生かし、次元を超えた自己改革を率先し合わなければならないのです。

　それは、私たちが武力や経済力などによる覇権や、消費の喜びを競いあうがごとき生き方を克服し、霊魂に基づく生態文明を創出し、清豊を目指すべきことを意味しています。つまり、人道という人類共通の価値観に基づき、古人（の知恵が編み出した文化）を尊重し、未来世代との公平を計る生き方、生態系の保守や保全に供しながら繁栄する生き方、そして創造の喜びを愛であう生き方を目指すことです。

Epilogue - The Dream of Noble Wealth

China introduced the "Five in One" policy at the 18th National People's Congress. I was moved when I learned that one of those points was the goal of "an ecological civilization." I learned from Liu Ying that it was written with the Chinese characters for "ecology" and "civilization." She explained further that the definition of this strategy is: Economics is fundamental, Politics is security, Culture is the soul of the nation, Society is a requirement, and Ecological civilization is the foundation. I was impressed because it seemed to me that these are tenets which should be subscribed to by all human beings. At the same time I felt a degree of frustration. There is a reason for that.

In 1986, I left my job, which offered me a fine income, to become a writer. My first book entitled *Vibgyor: Pioneers of a Post-consumer Society* saw the light of day immediately before the term "bubble economy" became trendy. The book was a call to action to create and transition to an age which will follow the industrial age. I refer to it as The Fourth Age. It urged all workers to become the flag bearers of **VIBGYOR** (the acronym for the colors of the rainbow from violet to red), a multifaceted color spectrum of talents. Sadly, those who were intoxicated with the bubble economy paid no attention.

In keeping with my apprehensions, eventually our industrial society began laying off white collar workers and blue collar workers who had monotone skills, and the movement toward industrial civilization began in earnest in many countries, including China. It was then that the Englishman, William Morris made his famous prediction that industrial society would produce a class of people who are slave to their wages, and would become even more wretched than farm slaves or medieval serfs.

Subsequently, I was invited to be the president of a women's junior college, which was facing serious enrollment issues, and my chief mission was the revitalization of the school. There I spread my own philosophy with the phrase, "Be the third cat!" Ten years later when I left the job, departments across all disciplines exceeded their enrollment quotas. Our students recommended our college as "a great school" to students at their former high schools and to others considering college.

Be the Third Cat
(Sankei News Column: "In Favor of Self-sufficiency March 3, 2006, Title: "The Third Cat")

It was the time of year when we were busy getting ready for the incoming class of students. I recall giving a pep talk to the students saying, "What number cat do you want to be?" And they all knew what I meant without further explanation, because I had lectured on it in my Environmentalism course.

"It is the ordinary cat that thinks the person who gives them a fish is kind. Actually, that is the person to fear. They are liable to make cats prone to forgetting how to catch fish. If that is so, can the person who teaches the cat how to fish be considered a kind person?" Here is the continuation of the story.

"But wait. This person should be feared as well. We need to realize that that person causes the depletion of our natural resources. I want you all be the third cat who has the vision to see that the person who teaches you the ecology of fish is truly the kindest person. I want you to be the smart cat who understands the secret of how to live in your environment along side fish, allowing them to flourish, as well as securing your own happiness.

The first cat is the cat which emerged from an agrarian society. The second cat is the cat that industrial society targeted ruthlessly. I urged my students to become the third cat which will take into consideration ecological systems in preparation for the post-industrial advent of the Fourth Age.

With this in mind, I was moved by the "Five in One" policy in China, and simultaneously I thought it unfortunate that I did not refer to the "Fourth Age" as the "Ecology Age."

The Ecology Age will pave the way for Ecology Civilization, but I am certain that the determining factor here will be a culture which values "spirit." Human beings bear the burden of issues they must overcome as they move from an industrial civilization to an ecological civilization, and "spirit" will become a key factor. This is one of the things I address in my book *The Next Way of Living* under the heading, "The Terrifying Nature of Civilization and the Importance of Culture."

Xi Jingping, China's president and chairman of the national congress, echoed these sentiments in his address to the 2017 National People's Congress. "The unusual socialist political system of China is an awe-inspiring creation. We are endowed with the confidence and ability to contribute to the progress of political civilization for all humankind." Indeed, it is the time when we must overcome any differences we might have in politics, religion or skin color, and stand together shoulder to shoulder to face our common enemy.

That enemy is what inhabits the hearts and minds of all of us in this industrial civilization who originally ventured out of Africa many millennia ago and dispersed over the face of the earth. To put it more concisely, this would be the overemphasis of Adam Smith's "invisible hand of self-interested action." We must reconsider the fact that we possess one "other hand" as well, and take the initiative to demonstrate to each other how to use that hand effectively and fully so as to affect a personal revolution, which exceeds conventional ideas of dimension.

We must now move beyond military or economic supremacy and a competition for the pleasure of consumption, and rather engage in creating an Ecology Civilization based on spiritual supremacy with a goal of noble wealth. In other words, we honor the culture which gave rise to the wisdom of the ancients, based on the common values of all humanity, and strive toward a way of life that promises equality for future generations, prosperity while maintaining the protection and conservation of our ecosystems, and a life which embraces the joy of creativity.

后记～生态文明的梦想～

中国在"第18次全国人民代表大会"中公布"五位一体"的政策，其中之一是"eco文明"。这个新闻让我很感动。刘颖女士告诉我用中文写是"生态文明"。并讲解了一下这个政策的具体内容："经济建设是根本，政治建设是保证，文化建设是灵魂，社会建设是条件，生态文明建设是基础。"我认为这些是全人类都要重视的标语，铭刻在我的心里。同时也有些遗憾，为什么呢？

1986年我与条件优越的公司告别，专心写作。处女作《大量消费社会的旗手们》问世的时期正好是"泡沫经济"这个词语流行之前。作品的主旨是创造工业时代以后的"第四时代"，提倡向新时代的转换，呼吁劳动者成为下个时代绚丽多彩的旗手=VIBGYOR（7色彩虹之意）。可惜的是，这个理念没有被开始沉醉于泡沫经济的人们所理睬。

不久就发生了令人畏惧的事，工业社会开始解雇（驱逐）单色的白领和蓝领。同时期，以中国为首的很多国家都虎视眈眈地向工业文明进军。那时候的我想起19世纪中期在英国，威廉·莫里斯（William Morris）留下的预言："工业社会产生的工资劳动者会比农业社会的奴隶和中世纪的农奴命运更加悲惨。"

此后，我接到一所女子短期大学的招聘。使命是复兴学校，改善招生不够的危机。当然，我大声呼吁自己的理论"学习第三只猫"，10年后我离开大学的时候，那时全学系的入学人数都超过了规定人数。听说在校生毕业时向自己母校的学生极力推荐："这个学校很好，你们来吧！"

～学习第三只猫～

现在正是准备迎接新生的繁忙季节。所以让我想起以前经常提醒学生们："你们想做第几只猫？"

因为在"环境论"的课上给学生们讲过这个故事，所以只凭一句话她们就明白我的意思。"如果认为总给自己鱼吃的人是好人，那它只是一般的猫。实际那个人很可怕，因为这样猫可能会忘了怎样去捉鱼。那么教猫怎样捉鱼的人是好人吗？"

这个问题的答案是："他也不是好人，这种人也很可怕。大家要知道这样会导致资源缺乏。我希望大家能够看清事情的真相，把鱼的生态教给自己的人才是真正的好人。你们要做第三只猫，学会怎样和鱼相处，怎样繁殖鱼让自己也过得幸福。在大家生活的环境里悟出这些道理，做一只聪明的猫。"（以下省略）

（产经新闻专栏"建议自给自足"2006年3月3日原题"第三只猫"）

第一只猫是农业社会的产物。第二只猫是工业社会贪婪追寻物质的丑态。我呼吁学生们要准备迎接"工业时代"以后的"第四时代"的到来，做第三只能够顾虑生态系的猫。

所以我看到中国"五位一体"这个全人类共同的课题非常感动。同时也感到十分惋惜，为什么自己没有想到把"第四时代"叫做"生态时代"呢？生态文明经过开辟进入生态时代，我确信它的依据出于将"文化"定位于"灵魂"。人类在从工业文明转移到"生态文明"的过程中，有一个必须克服的课题。那就是不可缺少灵魂。这个想法在我的著作《崭新的人生》的小标题"文明的恐怖和文化的重要性"里也提过。这是"生态文明时代"转换中人类存在的最大课题。

这个认识与习近平国家主席在2017年共产党人民代表大会中曾经指出的"具有中国特色的社会主义政治制度是伟大的创造。我们已经准备好为人类政治文明的进步做贡献的自信和能力。"产生共鸣。我们先不追究习近平思想的是非，但是现在必须超越某个主义和宗教以及肤色不同的阻碍，一起面对人类共同的敌人。

这个敌人活在我们这些居住工业文明群里的人心里。它是从5万年前的非洲启程，现在试图遍地球各地的现代人类。简单地说，它是亚当·斯密（Adam Smith）所说的"属于看不见的手-自爱心"的偏重。我们要重新认识到还有一只手，应该有效地去利用。相互监督，一起超过立场改革自我。

我们还应该放弃出自武力和经济的霸权，远离攀比消费喜悦的生活，创造以灵魂为基础的生态文明。这意味着以"清丰"为目标，也就是以人类共同的价值观"人道"为基础，尊重古人积累的智慧，生活上要考虑到是否对未来的下一代公平。在繁荣的同时保护和保全生态系，以热爱创造的喜悦为人生的目标。

这里谈到的"尊重古人积累的智慧，生活上要考虑到是否对未来的下一代公平"是我期待习近平政权的一个根据，希望大家去探讨。儒教的思想，不只现代的人，过去的人和未来的人都应该同样善待。

爱永远农园也是将"古人的智慧"和"近代科学的成果"灵活运用在一起的。它的做法不但能让现在的人接受，同时不断追求未来的人也一样能够以此为乐地生活。这个意识本来是从母亲那里领悟的，以后自己又巩固起来。

民主主义不只现在如此，它始终轻易允许个人主义的放纵，把虚伪当作体面的人可以自由自在地横行于世。这次酷暑中发生的各种天灾人祸也许就出于这些累积起来的教训。

习近平以后由于中国的自由化现代派的抬头，也许会遭到冷落。此外，人们重新认识儒教，呼吁复活它的必要性的人一定也会抬头。我想后者必定胜利。如果失败，这个地球也就面临毁灭了。

あとがき

　この一文を私は4者の共著だと思っています。劉穎さんと、劉穎さんが中国文をつくる上で参考にした英文の作者・エリザベス アームストロングさん、そしてもう1人、喜田真弓さんです。彼女をエリザベスさんに紹介したのは私ですが、この2人は日米の文化などを深く踏まえて英訳し、さらに劉さんは日中の文化などを深く踏まえて中国訳しました。その過程で私はこの3人から多大な贈物を得ています。それは後に触れる共感と勇気です。

　エリザベスさんと劉さんの2人と私の関係は、既に少し触れましたが、喜田さんの紹介もここで加えたく思います。彼女は、ビル・トッテンさん（株式会社アシストの創業者で、現会長）の片腕です。トッテンさんは数々の日本語の著作を世に送り出していますが、そのすべてが彼女の手を得て日本文になっています。そのありようを知り、トッテンさんの親友だと自任している私は、彼女に助言を要請したのです。

　なぜこの3人には、翻訳や助言という無償の協力に応じてもらえたのか。私には思いあたるフシがあります。この一文は、過去四半世紀分の私のコラムをつなぎ合わせたようなものですが、これらコラムの源泉である次の「生きる指針」がそのフシでしょう。

"地球人としての認識"の下に、
"生態系への復帰"を宣言し、
"不可逆的な生活システムとの決別"を誓う。

　この指針は、1973年に誕生しています。オイルショックを機に、私の心に言い聞かせるために私が創りました。その後、1986年から「アイトワの理念」として、その喫茶店頭で公表し、1988年には処女作で「ポスト消費社会の旗手・ビブギオールカラー」の理念として紹介しています。そして今も、何かに躓くと私は読み直します。なぜなら、そうしてきたことがトッテンさんと私をつないだようですし、他にも多々未来が微笑みかけて来るような実感を得させたり、良き縁に巡り合わせたりしてきたからです。

　実は、トッテンさんには、その著作などに触れて共感した私の方から近づきました。その後、彼はアイトワのこの理念が形作らせた庭に共感してくださった。この2人の共鳴はおのずと喜田さんの存在を浮かび上がらせた、というわけです。

　昨今の世の中は武力や経済力などによる覇権を競いかねない勢いです。これは地球にとっては自殺幇助でしょう。時あたかも、中国は五位一体を打ち出しました。ならば、江戸時代という文化と実績を有する日本が割って入らなければならない時ではないでしょうか。

　こうした思いを、ここに紹介した人たちの協力を得て一書に出来ました。ちなみに、私たち夫婦は、エリザベスをアメリカの長女と呼んでいますし、劉さんを日中民間外交官と思っています。そして、トッテンさんと私は、喜田さんに庭仕事の話が込み入った時や養蜂の師匠を訪ねる時も世話になっています。こうした3人に私は助けられたわけで、共感と勇気以上のものを与えられたものと受け止めています。

Afterword

I consider myself just one of four authors of this publication. The Chinese was done by Liu Ying, the English by Elizabeth Armstrong, assisted by Mayumi Kita. Mayumi and Elizabeth bringing to their deep understanding of Western culture to their translation, as Liu Ying brought her deep understanding of Chinese culture to the Chinese version. In the process of working together, I received inestimable gifts from all three of them. These gifts are empathy and courage.

I have mentioned my relationship with Elizabeth and Liu Ying, and here I will add some background about Mayumi Kita. She is the right-hand person to Bill Totten, the founder and Chairman of the Board of K.K. *Ashisuto*, a Japanese software company. He has written many books about his philosophy of business and life, and all of them were translated into Japanese by Mayumi. In my interactions with Bill, I learned of Mayumi's translation expertise and sought her advice.

Why did these three people offer their translation expertise and advice *pro bono?* One thing in particular comes to mind. This publication, which is the culmination of the columns I have written over the past quarter century, provides this opportunity to share my life philosophy and the source of all these columns.

I, as a resident of the planet,
declare a return to oneness with the Earth's ecological system
and pledge to bid farewell to a life system that is irreversible.

I first wrote out this personal creed in 1973 at the time of the oil shocks, and referred to it as a constant reminder of what is important. Subsequently, in 1986 I adopted it as "**aightowa**'s philosophy", and in 1988 published it as the central philosophy of my first book *Vibgyor: Pioneers of a Post-consumer Society*. Even today, whenever I falter I re-read this pledge to the planet. It has done many wonderful things for me. It has brought me together with Bill Totten, allowed me a solid sense of what multiple futures will smile upon, and has blessed me with fortuitous encounters.

I read Bill Totten's books and was so moved by them that I took the initiative to approach him. In return, he graciously expressed a spirit of kinship with our eco-garden, the physical manifestation of **aightowa**'s philosophy. The resonance between Bill and myself brought to light Mayumi's presence.

Looking at the big picture, we can see that the current momentum of US-China relations could very well escalate into a competition for military and economic hegemony. This would be akin to assisted suicide for the planet. It is also precisely at this moment when China unveiled its "Five-in-One" policy. Surely this is the moment when Japan, fortified with its Edo-period culture and accomplishments, must step up and mediate.

These are the thoughts that I have brought together in this publication with the cooperation of Liu Ying, Elizabeth and Mayumi. I couldn't be more fortunate. They have given me gifts which go beyond both empathy and courage.

后记

我觉得这本书是4个人共同的著作。中文翻译刘颖，以及她在翻译时参考的英文是由英文翻译伊利莎白担任的。此外，还有一个人是喜田真弓。我把她介绍给伊利莎白，她们一起依据日本和美国的文化背景进行翻译，刘颖也同样在对比中日文化的情况下翻译成中文。在这个过程，我从三位翻译那儿学习到不少东西。那就是其后我要讲的同感和勇气。

伊利莎白、刘颖和我的关系以前已经讲过。这里加上喜田真弓的介绍。她是比尔托滕（Bill Totten）K.K.（ASI-ST）的创始人（现任会长）的左膀右臂。比尔托滕出版了很多日语版的著作，这些都是喜田真弓翻译的。我了解她的才能，作为比尔托滕的好友，自己的这本书也请她给予帮助。

为什么这三个人能无偿的为我翻译，而且给予宝贵的意见呢？其中的原因我很清楚。这篇文章可以把我过去二十五年的散文连接起来。它来源于以下"活着的指针"。

在"作为地球人类的认识"下、
宣布"复归生态系"、
发誓"和不可反抗的生活系统诀别"

这个指针诞生在1973年。是发生石油危机时，我在心里悟出的道理，也是为了告诫自己的。此后1986年，作为"爱永远农园的理念"，在农园咖啡店的店头正式发表。1988年的处女作《大量消费社会的旗手们》里也曾介绍这个理念。现在当我受到什么挫折的时候，就会把它再读一遍。因为这样做让我和比尔托滕相识，还得到很多未来向我们微笑的实感，并且结下很多良缘。

实际和比尔托滕的相识，是我读他的著作感到共鸣后去接近他的。那以后，他对我建设爱永远农园的理念产生了同感。这样我们两个人的共鸣突出了喜田真弓的存在。

无论过去还是现在，美国和中国随时都显露出以武力和经济力量竞争霸权的趋势。这对地球来说等于是帮助自杀的行为。时期正赶上中国推出"五位一体"的政策。那么这个时代日本也应该乘机加入其中，因为我们国家具有江户时代引以为荣的文化功绩。

这些想法在介绍作品的人们的协助下完成此书，我感到十分幸福。我们夫妻把伊丽莎白看作美国的长女，刘颖的活动使我们觉得她是中日民间的外交官。我和比尔托滕先生谈论庭院工作的时候和养蜂师傅访问的时候都由喜田女士仲介帮助。是她们三人给了我援助，不但让我获得同感和勇气，还有其他很多宝贵的东西。

著者・翻訳者／略歴

作者・森孝之：
エコロジスト、アイトワ代表。京都工芸繊維大学、伊藤忠商事、伊藤忠ファッションシステム・チーフプランナー、ワールド社長室長・取締役　子会社ノーブルグー社長、大垣女子短期大学学長などを経て今日に至る。著書、『人と地球に優しい企業』講談社、『「想い」を売る会社』日本経済新聞社、『京都嵐山エコトピアだより』小学館など。1986年アイトワ設立。日本エッセイストクラブ会員、日本ペンクラブ会員。

Author: Takayuki Mori is an ecologist and owner of **aightowa**, opened in 1986. He graduated from The Kyoto Institute of Technology and joined the trading company, Itochu. Subsequently, he worked for Itochu Fashion System as their strategic planner and then took the position of chief of staff and planning at the fashion company, World, Co. Ltd. Following this he was appointed president of the apparel company, NOBLEGOÛT. He left industry and became president of Ogaki Women's College until his retirement. Among his publications are *Businesses for People and the World* (Kodansha), *Conscience Business* (Nikkei Inc.), *The Kyoto-Arashiyama Ecotopia* (Shogakkan). He is a member of the Japan Essayist Club and the Japan PEN Club.

作者・森孝之：生态学者、爱永远农园代表。担任京都工艺纤维大学、伊藤忠商事、伊藤忠服饰系统·设计主任、株式会社（世界WORLD）经理助理·董事，分公司Noblegoo经理、大垣女子短期大学校长等职位。著作《有益人类和地球的企业》讲谈社出版、《传播思想的公司》日本经济新闻社出版、《京都岚山理想乐园信息》小学馆出版等。1986年设立爱永远农园、日本散文作家俱乐部会员、日本文笔协会会员。

英訳者・エリザベス・アームストロング：
大学時代に日本へ留学。卒業後、日本企業での勤務経験も持つ。1999年より米国バックネル大学東亜研究学部で教鞭をとり、2017年から教授。専門は日本語教育及び翻訳論。英訳書に寺山修司作『赤糸で縫いとじられた物語』『僕が狼だった頃』がある。森夫妻との長年に渡る付き合いを誇りに思い、宝物だと思っている。

English Translator: Elizabeth Armstrong has been teaching at Bucknell University in the United States since 1999. Her areas of focus are Japanese language and translation studies. She has published two translations of work by Terayama Shūji: *The Crimson Thread of Abandon* (2014), and *When I Was a Wolf* (2018). She first came to Japan as a student and subsequently worked in Japanese industry as well. She is proud of her long and treasured friendship with Takayuki and Sayoko Mori.

英译/伊丽莎白·阿姆斯斗龙（Elizabeth Armstrong）：自1999年在美国巴克内尔大学的东亚研究系任教。专攻日语教育和翻译论。英文翻译作品有寺山修司的『用红线编织的故事』(2014)以及《那时候我是狼》(2018)。学生时代就屡次访日，并在日企就过职。特别与本书作者森孝之夫妻的长年来往，给她留下宝贵的印象，并引以为豪。

英訳助言・喜田真弓：
1984年株式会社アシストに入社。社長室、広報部を経て現在　経営企画本部において広報関係およびビル・トッテン（アシスト創業者）の業務支援に携わる。訳書に、ビル・トッテン『日本はアメリカの属国ではない』（ごま書房）がある。

English Consultant: Mayumi Kita joined K.K. *Ashisuto* in 1984. She worked in the President's Office and in Public Relations, and is now a member of the Management Planning Group. In addition to these duties, she also works as a research assistant for Bill Totten, founder and Chairman of K.K. *Ashisuto*. She produced the Japanese translation of Bill Totten's book *Japan is not an American Vassal State* (Goma Shobo).

英译参谋/喜田真弓：1984年就职于股份公司ASI-ST。做过经理室、宣传部的工作，现在参与经营计划本部的宣传以及公司创业者比尔托滕（BILL TOTTEN）的业务支援。翻译作品有《日本不是美国的属国》比尔托滕著（GOMA书房出版）。

中国語訳・劉穎：
1986年来日、中国残留孤児三世。大阪大学卒業後、語学講師、翻訳者、通訳と幅広く活躍。2008年NPO法人滋賀日中文化交流センターを設立し、多文化共生推進事業に関わるなど、現在佛教大学の文学研究員。翻訳作品は今関信子の児童文学推薦図書『小犬の裁判はじめます』（童心社）、メルマガ『日中翻訳鑑賞』がある。

Chinese translator: Liu Ying came to Japan in 1986, and is the third generation of a Japanese war orphan. After graduating from Osaka University, she has been broadly active as a language instructor, translator and interpreter. In 2008 she established the NPO Shiga Japan/China Cultural Exchange Center, and has been involved in promoting harmony among diverse cultures. Currently, she is a researcher at Bukkyo University. She has published *The Puppy's Court Case* (Huaxia Press), a translation on the list of recommended children's books.

中译译者/刘颖：1986年来日本、中国战争孤儿三世。大阪大学毕业后从事外语讲师、翻译等工作。2008年成立NPO法人滋贺日中文化交流中心，为多文化共生推进事业做贡献。现在是佛教大学的研究员。翻译作品有今关信子的儿童文学推荐图书《小狗裁判开始了》（华夏出版社）、网络杂志《中日翻译鉴赏》等。

未来が微笑みかける生き方 〜 AI 時代の自給自足 〜
Life the Future Smiles Upon - Self-sufficiency in the AI Age
未来向我们微笑的人生〜人工智能时代的自给自足〜

2019 年 1 月 5 日　第 1 版 1 刷発行

著　者　　森　孝之
英訳者　　エリザベス・アームストロング
英訳助言　喜田真弓
中国語訳　劉穎
編　集　　浅井潤一
レイアウト　吉川智香子
写　真　　森　小夜子　（一部を除く）

　　　　　アイトワ　森　孝之
　　　　　〒 616-8396　京都市右京区嵯峨小倉山山本町 1
　　　　　1,Yamamotocho, Ogurayama, Saga, Ukyo-ku, KYOTO JAPAN
　　　　　TEL 075-881-5321　FAX 075-861-5607
　　　　　aightowa@cpost.plala.or.jp

発行所　　株式会社　亥辰舎
　　　　　〒 612-8438　京都市伏見区深草フチ町 1-3
　　　　　TEL 075-644-8131　FAX 075-644-5225
　　　　　http://www.ishinsha.com

印刷所　　土山印刷株式会社
定　価　　本体 1,800 円＋税
　　　　　ISBN978-4-904850-80-0

ⓒ ISHINSHA 2019 Printed in Japan
本誌掲載の写真、記事の無断転載を禁じます。
不得擅自转载本书的照片和文章。